G R JORDAN

Seoras, They Shot Him

Seoras Macleod Mysteries #1

"It's only murder if there's a body; otherwise, it's a missing person."

ANONYMOUS

Contents

Preface

Welcome to the start of the Seoras Macleod Mysteries! For those in the know, Seoras started his life in books in the highly successful Highlands and & Detective Thrillers series which is still continuing despite his leaving. You can check the series out here!

Having retired from his day job as a DCI in the Scottish police force, Seoras and his partner Jane are off to see the world. But a decent man can't just step away when bad things happen and they are soon embroiled in many mysteries but without the resources and authority Seoras was so used to. I hope you find these tales as enjoyable as the Seoras's "day job" series has been.

Acknowledgments

To Ken, Jean, Colin, Evelyn, John and Rosemary for your work in bringing this novel to completion, your time and effort is deeply appreciated.

Books by G R Jordan

Seoras Macleod Mysteries

1. Seoras, They Shot Him!
2. Seoras, Grab the Kid! (Feb 2026)
3. Seoras, White Smoke Ahead! (Apr 2026)

The Highlands and Islands Detective series (Crime)

1. Water's Edge
2. The Bothy
3. The Horror Weekend
4. The Small Ferry
5. Dead at Third Man
6. The Pirate Club
7. A Personal Agenda
8. A Just Punishment
9. The Numerous Deaths of Santa Claus
10. Our Gated Community
11. The Satchel
12. Culhwch Alpha
13. Fair Market Value
14. The Coach Bomber

Kirsten Stewart Thrillers (Thriller)

Jac Moonshine Thrillers

1. Jac's Revenge
2. Jac for the People
3. Jac the Pariah

Siobhan Duffy Mysteries

1. A Giant Killing
2. Death of the Witch
3. The Bloodied Hands
4. A Hermit's Death

The Contessa Munroe Mysteries (Cozy Mystery)

1. Corpse Reviver
2. Frostbite
3. Cobra's Fang

The Patrick Smythe Series (Crime)

1. The Disappearance of Russell Hadleigh
2. The Graves of Calgary Bay
3. The Fairy Pools Gathering

Austerley & Kirkgordon Series (Fantasy)

1. Crescendo!
2. The Darkness at Dillingham
3. Dagon's Revenge
4. Ship of Doom

Supernatural and Elder Threat Assessment Agency (SETAA) Series (Fantasy)

1. Scarlett O'Meara: Beastmaster

Island Adventures Series (Cosy Fantasy Adventure)

1. Surface Tensions

Dark Wen Series (Horror Fantasy)

1. The Blasphemous Welcome
2. The Demon's Chalice

Chapter 01

'Would you look at that?'

'Look at it? I can barely keep my eyes open,' said Seoras. 'Flying all the way out to the Seychelles, and then, another flight.'

He felt a dig in the ribs. Jane Hislop, his partner, was looking out to the island below which the small aircraft was circling.

'There's like a tiny strip down there, for a runway.'

'A runway? Barely an airport. I know you wanted it to be a surprise,' said Seoras, 'but you could have prepped me. You could have told me it would be—'

'Would you shut up?' said Jane. 'Shut up and look down here.' She felt a set of arms reaching around her, and Seoras hugged in tight. He was looking past her, through the window, and down to the blue sea below.

'It's very clear, isn't it? We had a clear sea back on Lewis. Some days, it was—'

'They were a lot bloody colder on Lewis,' said Jane. 'Here, we've got the sand, we've got the sun. It's even a big enough island for you to go for a walk if you need to. But we're going to have a relaxing time. I didn't get a tour where you'd have to run around, where you'd feel obliged to look at things. We're

1

just going to camp out, the two of us, together.'

'Camp out. You never told me there'd be camping.'

'It's just an expression,' said Jane, reaching down to the hands that were wrapped around her to squeeze them. 'They do these beach huts. Well, they say beach huts. They're just amazing.'

'How did we afford to get out here?'

'We can afford it, rightly. I have a little money. You have a bit of money. There are only the two of us, and we don't spend an awful lot. Shut up and look at that view.'

Seoras smiled. Was this his perfect holiday? Probably not. Lying on a beach, scorching sun. He liked to think of himself more as a man of action, but in truth, he could do with just doing nothing for a while, relaxing, as Jane said. The two of them could do with it. They never seem to have got time together, not truly, not without the call of the job.

Seoras had recently retired from Police Scotland, having worked the last years of his career in Inverness. Detective Chief Inspector looking after the murder team, an arts team, and also a cold-case unit, but they'd taken him away from his principal job a year or two before. He had been happiest when he'd been a DI running the murder team.

How do you become happiest investigating the darkest side of people? This is where I should be happiest, he thought. He lent his head into the back of Jane's. He had once had a wife called Hope, and they'd lived on the Isle of Lewis together. But she died in the sea at home, a choice she'd made. It had taken him a long time to get past that, and Jane had been a big part of his moving on. He'd met her after he'd come up to Inverness on a case, and he'd convinced her to stay with him. Now, owning a house on the Black Isle, north of the Kessock Bridge, they were going to enjoy life together. He'd hung up his policeman's hat,

2

or fedora as he had worn, and now he'd picked up a new hat.

Well actually, he was wearing the fedora that they'd given him at his retirement do. It was much funkier than the old one. That was the word, wasn't it? Funky? He didn't know these days, for Seoras wasn't good at the modern stuff. He'd also given up the ties. No longer would he wear a tie and shirt. No more would he investigate as that rather dour-looking inspector.

It was still in him—of course, it was. But there was another side to him here. A side that realised that this was his chance at another life—a life with the woman before him.

Jane had been through a lot. She'd been attacked because of his job in the past. But she'd always stood by him, never interfering but proud. And now he wanted to give back some of that time. He wanted to make the rest of their life together perfect. Jane needed to be happy, for she made him happy.

'We'd better sit back; we're about to land,' said Jane. Seoras leaned back in his seat, but his hand went across and took hers. She was smiling as they landed, her man with her, the way she wanted him, unfettered by responsibility.

It was a small plane with only twelve passengers. When they got off, they were greeted by what probably would have been called a tour guide, although they looked a lot less formal than that.

'Mr and Mrs Macleod, is it?'

'No,' said Jane, 'we're just partners. That's Mr Macleod.'

'Seoras and Jane,' said Seoras, stepping forward and shaking the man's hand.

'If you let me grab your bags, we'll take you over to the Jeep, and run you down to your accommodation. I hope you're going to be thrilled here at Pining Seas.'

'Pining Seas?' asked Seoras. 'Why is it called that?'

'Oh, the island owner, he kept pining to come back here, so he called it the Pining Seas. Maybe I'll take you on a tour of the island first. That would probably be useful. There are a few areas which are out of bounds for guests and also for any visitors. It's not a completely private island. We have people who do come and visit us, who don't stay in our accommodation. However, being where it is, out in the middle of the ocean, with no one around for miles, we do like to say it's our private island.'

The man laughed and walked off to find the bags. Seoras stood with his fedora on his head, gazing around. There was a woman who had just got off the plane. She looked rather strange and kept fidgeting, going down to her phone. He wondered what she was doing. *There are a couple of pieces of paper sticking out of her handbag. She obviously doesn't want anybody to see them too closely. She—*

'Stop it,' said Jane bluntly.

'What?' asked Seoras.

'She's not a case. We are not trying to find out what is wrong, okay? We are just here to enjoy ourselves. Stop looking at people as if they've got something to hide.'

'Well, everybody's got something to hide.'

'No, they haven't. There are genuinely nice people in this world. You need to learn that.'

'I was only looking. I said nothing,' said Seoras.

'You don't have to. I appreciate that mind's going to take time to wind down.'

'I hope it will not wind down.'

'Okay, look to focus on a different subject,' said Jane. She took his hands. 'Focus on this subject,' she said. She stood

4

slightly smaller than him, and he bent down, kissing her on the lips. When he broke off, she smiled. 'Well, that was very brave. Public show of affection like that.'

'If you're going to tease me, I'll stop doing it,' he said.

'Whenever you're ready,' said a voice. They turned to see the young man who had met them sitting in a Jeep. When they walked over, Seoras went to let Jane go in the front. She shook her head.

'Go on,' she said. 'You'll be keen to look everywhere and know everything.'

'No,' he said.

'Yes,' she said. 'It's going to take time to refocus. But look everywhere. Know everything about the island. It's fine. That's why I picked it. There's more than just a beach hut and sand.'

'Oh, there's a lot more than that,' said the driver.

As they drove out of the little airport, basically a strip of tarmac with a small building and a few hangars, Seoras looked around him. There was a flat area they were on, but they were soon heading up towards some hills. As they crossed over them, they drove down until he saw several large fences. There was a building beyond it. It wasn't vast, but it was significant, like a small secondary school. There were a few guards around, and one or two of them carried guns.

'Now, I don't want you to be alarmed,' said the man driving. 'This is the private end of the island, very much private.'

'What is it?' asked Seoras.

'It's a research facility. It's off-limits to guests because of the research that goes on inside. There are people who would want to know what that research is.'

'I assume it's all legal and legitimate.'

'Well, of course it is,' said the man, laughing. 'But it's a great place to do it, because we're so far away from the rest of the world. It prevents others who would look in. Espionage is quite normal in a lot of research fields, finding out what others know. I don't know if you're aware of the crimes that go on.'

Seoras looked away, but he could feel Jane's eyes burning into the back of his head. *Don't say. Don't tell them.* Her voice was there in his head.

'Well, the trouble is that people come and they try all sorts of things. Trying to steal from you after all the hard work that's gone into it. The island's owner, the governor, as we like to call him, likes to be quiet about his business. But you can see clearly where you can't go. All the gates and, to be honest, you don't really want to be up this end. There's nothing to see in this little alcove of the island except the facility. He made it that way so it would be remote, quiet, and people wouldn't be bothered by it. The chief town is at the other end of the island. There's one or two smaller little places to visit, and we'll show you the large lagoon in the middle.'

The man spun the wheel, and the dusty track blew up a cloud screen that meant Seoras looking back could barely see the facility in their wake. He did see Jane smiling at him and mouthing a 'well done,' sarcastic in the extreme. His hand shot up, however, to his fedora hat. The sun was beating down now, and he could feel the heat, making him glad of the hat on his head. Jane, however, was basking in warmth.

The vehicle cruised through a couple of small, almost villages, with some local shops and dwellings.

'Who lives here then?' asked Seoras.

'Well, those who live on the island and who work here. Some of us live in the town; some of us work up at the facility. The ones from the facility are a lot closer, in these outlying villages. The rest of us live down in the Port's Bay because there's more going on. That's where you'll see a few of the clubs and restaurants.'

'Nightclubs,' said Seoras.

'Not nightclubs. We have our own types of music here. There's dancing, but it's more informal. I think you'll like it. You look like the dancing sort of man.'

Jane burst out laughing in the back seat. 'He does a mean karaoke, but his sparring partner's not with him,' she said.

She was referring to DI Clarissa Urquhart, who had forcibly got Seoras up to sing karaoke at a few of their work events. Seoras rolled his eyes.

They drove into Port's Bay. It had small apartments, and then a few larger houses, swimming pools on the outside. At the far end, however, there was a congregation of different beach huts, leading straight on to the sand and the surf. The man stopped at one of them before jumping out and pointing.

'And this is yours, two hundred yards from the sea. Nobody will come close to your hut. The rules are that if you want to go onto the beach, it's just beyond that line there you can see marked by the stones. So beyond that, there is free rein for anybody to use the beach. This bit here—that's yours.'

He marched up with a key and opened the door. Returning, he grabbed their bags and then led them inside. The interior was stunning, with modern conveniences here, there, and everywhere. While it wasn't enormous, it was more than big enough for the two of them. The bedroom had a large double bed Seoras thought he might get lost in, as well as walk-in wardrobes. Their bags were set down for them inside the hut, and the man ran them through a few of the electrical devices.

Seoras was delighted to see there was a coffee machine.

'What sort of coffee do you have on the island?'

'There's a coffee shop just in the town, stocked with some good stuff. I'm no expert myself.'

'Oh, he is. It'd better be good,' said Jane. 'It'd better be blooming good.'

Soon they were left alone, and Jane gave him a hug. Seoras hugged her back.

'Right,' she said. 'Have your wander.'

'What?' he said.

'You're going to want to know what that coffee shop is like. So get to it. Check it out and then come back. We're going out for dinner tonight. But first, I'm going to lie on the beach for an hour.'

She let go and headed to the bedroom. By the time he'd got his hat on and was about to head out the door, she'd emerged again in a swimsuit that was cut a lot tighter than the ones she wore at the swimming pool.

'Do you like it?' she said.

'Wow!'

She ran up and kissed him. 'That's the correct response. Keep that up and you never know your luck might be in.'

She left through the front door, and he watched her padding down to the beach. She had no towel with her and just plopped herself on the sand. That was Jane. She just did things. Impulsive at times—a live wire—but she took him out of himself, and he felt good. This was going to be his life now. This was going to be him and her. Seoras marched off to the coffee shop because that was absolutely what he needed to do.

Entering the shopping area, he found it to be quite busy.

People were rushing here and there for groceries, and some people were drinking at bars. As he entered the coffee shop, the smell of a brew that he liked hit him with full force.

'Cortado,' he said, smiling at the girl behind the counter.

'Where have you come in from?' she asked. She had dark skin, long ringlets of black hair and could only have been in her early twenties. Seoras thought she was beautiful looking as he replied, 'Scotland.'

'I thought you looked a bit pasty,' she said, turning to make his cortado. When she served it to him, he took a drink in front of her, then gave her a smile. *They could make coffee*, he thought. *Good!* He settled down in a seat close to the window and watched the world go by.

People were marching here and there, and all seemed to be good in the world. Most seemed to be here to enjoy themselves. He could see several yachts moored off the shore. Seoras wondered what sort of money some of these people had. Yet there were workers, people here to provide for the island and for the services within it. As he finished his cortado, he thought, *this will be good. Jane'll like this, and so will I. She's good, clever at what she does. She had picked the perfect holiday.*

Returning to their beach hut, Seoras entered and heard the shower running. He walked through to the ensuite, opened it up and marched straight in to where he saw Jane standing, showering. She opened her eyes.

'Well, that's subtle,' she said. 'The least you could do is get your gear off and get in there with me.'

'Thought we were going for dinner.'

'Doesn't mean you don't have to shower as well.'

He went to turn to get changed in the room, but he heard a shout.

'Oi,' she said. He turned back. 'Something wrong with the view?'

'Nothing,' he said.

Jane was washing her hair now. 'I saw some military personnel. Not guards, but military. Well, they looked like they had fatigues, only they were sandy coloured.'

'You told me not to be watching. You told me,' said Seoras, 'that I had to behave and not watch.'

'Well, I don't watch,' she said, 'so I'm allowed to. Besides, you will not criticise a woman you're going to take to dinner when she's standing in the shower in front of you.'

'No, I won't,' he said.

Jane stepped out of the shower, and he handed her a towel. She dried herself off. As he turned to walk through to the bedroom, she grabbed his hand and turned him back, wrapping herself around him.

'Got you to myself now,' she said.

'You have,' he said. 'You deserve it.'

'I deserve it. You're the lucky one.' She grinned at him.

Chapter 02

'**D**o I look all right?' asked Jane.

Seoras stared at the woman in front of him. She was wearing a dress that set off her hair, and while not being too tight—because the pair of them did have to acknowledge that they weren't in the flush of youth—certainly showed off her curves. *She looks stunning*, he thought, *vibrant, alive*.

His eye as a police detective over the years had taught him a lot, and he could see the interior of people from the outside. Jane oozed passion and drive despite the fact that she could be shy. She was bubbly, not because she was trying to cover up her shyness, but because that's the way she was. Mischievous, always looking to push you past your limits, and that's what he loved about her. And the dress was like this. She didn't look like someone trying to be twenty or thirty years her junior, but the dress just had a little punch about it. It made her look ten years younger than her actual age, but then again, to Jane, there was no such thing as age. She was just Jane.

He had been feeling his age recently. Retirement had come because of it. The body had struggled with the demands of the job, but his body felt alive now, looking at this woman in front of him. He stepped forward and kissed her gently on the lips.

'You looked amazing. Every curve, every wrinkle, every bit of you,' he said.

'Every wrinkle. You seriously just said, "every wrinkle."'

'Oh, you can't all have a body like me,' said Seoras. She poked him in the stomach, forcing him to double up.

'Oh, you will pay for that,' she said. As he stood back up, she smacked him on the backside. 'Out! Let's go!'

Jane had a grin on her face, though. She liked it, pulling out the banter in him. Working as a murder detective, he didn't get that many funny moments. There was a lot of seriousness. And that's how the Force had seen him. Sombre. But Jane had seen the other side of him, the side that had to be brought out. The side that wouldn't let go. It was a side that she loved.

It was slightly cooler now, but certainly nothing like the highlands of Scotland as they walked along the streets of Port's Bay. The road was dusty, but was a tarmac one, and there were plenty of people on the go tonight. There was music coming from certain bars, but the restaurant they went to had a large outdoor area. Jane gave their name, and they were taken to a table for two, close to a large dance floor. A band was playing, and Seoras could see Jane was almost itching to get up.

'We're eating first,' he said. 'I am hungry; we are eating. You haven't dragged me across the world to then not eat.'

'Well, eat then,' she said, as the menus were brought. The food was superb. Seoras had fish with rice, and though he couldn't quite place what the sauce over it was, it was delicious. Jane seemed happy with her chicken, and then afterwards, the chocolate dessert had arrived. A romantic one, shared for two, although Jane seemed to eat most of it. It was also a work of art. Jane drank a deep red wine, and Seoras could see her relax, the shyness going away. It was a shyness that lots of people didn't see within her. Jane had learned to take on the world, learned to brave it out, but when she relaxed, she truly was something.

Seoras didn't drink. He never had. Brought up on the Isle of Lewis, where alcohol was seen as evil, especially in the church he grew up in. He had just never been one for drinking. Jane told him he didn't need it, but he knew what his alcohol was. She was sitting across from him. Jane was the one who made him relax. She made him do those daft things in life she couldn't do without a quick shot.

The music suddenly became livelier. Several people jumped onto the dance floor. It was more of a sawdust area than a dance floor. Seoras was dragged up, and together the two of them danced. Not that they were outstanding dancers, but nobody seemed to care. Everyone was there for a good time, and he even tried dancing behind her, holding her around the waist. Who knew what they looked like? Who cared?

'Just let go,' she said to him, and he bent down and kissed her as they danced. She had loved that. Again, he had no idea what sort of figure he cut. He never would have done it back in Scotland. Not at a work's do. He'd got up and sung karaoke, but he wouldn't have done this. And yet she made him want to.

It must have been around one in the morning when they left the restaurant. Jane had taken her shoes off, though they weren't high heels. She couldn't have stood high heels these days. Even so, her flat sandals had ached, but the road was good enough that she could walk along it barefoot.

As they approached their beach hut, she pulled him away, veering off down to the shoreline. At first, she told him to take

13

off his shoes and his socks, and rolling his trousers up, they walked along. She started kicking water over him. He kicked it back. And then Jane dragged Seoras out past his knees. She kept going and he suddenly reached down and grabbed his wallet.

'Give me that,' she said, taking it off him and flinging it clear of the water onto the beach.

'You can't do that!'

'Shut up!'

Seoras could see the wine was talking. She wasn't slurring, but she'd gone past the stage of any inhibition. It was daring. It was reckless. And then they heard a sound coming down the beach—laughter. He felt his arm being pulled and the next second, Jane had pulled him down into the water. The two of them were left with only their heads left above it.

Again, it wasn't like Scotland. This water was warm. And he felt her arms go around him, holding him tight.

'Shush,' she said. 'Look at those two.'

There was a couple maybe fifty yards away. They were running into the sea without a stitch on them. They could only have been in their early twenties, and Jane whispered in his ear, 'Tomorrow night.'

He whispered back, 'I don't think my knees would run that quickly. I think I would have fallen over by now.'

He felt her poke him in the back. The young couple suddenly raced back out and off along the beach. Jane took his hand and led him back out of the water. He picked up his wallet, keeping it in his hand rather than putting it back in his sodden clothes.

'Quite hedonistic, isn't it?' he said.

'It's what?'

'It's very hedonistic. People are just doing what they want. I mean, you wouldn't get that back home, would you?'

'You wouldn't get people at one in the morning running into the water in the loch. No, you wouldn't,' said Jane. 'It's Baltic. You'd freeze to death.'

'Even so, if it were warm, they still wouldn't do it.'

'Don't tempt me, Seoras Macleod,' she said. He looked, and she was grinning. Then Seoras froze. She looked at him. 'What?'

He held a finger up to his mouth. Gently, he walked her close to another beach hut and stopped. There were voices coming from the other side of it. He peered around but could only see the back end of a Land Rover.

'You'd better sort it. You've made a mess, and he's not happy.' *The voice is harsh. An older man.*

'These things happen. These things happen, and you just have to take the hit. We can try to sort it out afterwards. But sometimes things don't go as planned.' *This is a younger voice. Maybe thirties*, Seoras thought.

'I'm telling you; he's pissed. He's absolutely pissed. If I were you, I wouldn't go up there.'

'How can I not go up there? You know what it's like. He tells you to go, you go. I'll talk my way out of it, don't worry. He'll see my side of it. We'll go and we'll sort this out.'

'They're coming. You realise they're coming. He wanted it for them. "It would make his day," he said. He doesn't say stuff like that.'

'He's just going to have to learn to live with it. There are things that go on out there. It's not an exact science. It's not simple, you know. Go with the flow, and sometimes the flow doesn't work. Sometimes you must have a second attempt or

15

a third attempt.'

'Well, he's not used to that,' said the older man. 'He's not used to that at all. For your sakes, I wouldn't go meet him.'

'You're full of it,' said the younger man. 'You always over-dramatise him. Say he's this, he's that. Since the first day we met, you've always said that. You act as if he's some sort of god. He just does whatever.'

'Well, sometimes he does. You haven't known him like I've known him.'

Seoras tried to creep round, but all he could see was the back of the Jeep. Jane was pulling at him, and he turned to look at her. She lifted her shoulders, questioning what he was doing. Again, he put his finger up to his lips.

'Well, that's all you're getting from me. I'm off. I'll see him tomorrow.'

'Get on a plane and don't come back.'

'How can I not come back? This is what I do, my living. This is how I earn money.'

'I'm just telling you. Bravado only gets you so far. He can see through that.'

The Jeep started up, and Seoras saw the back end of it driving away briefly before it was fully behind the beach hut. He heard footsteps going away as well. And then he felt Jane tug him again.

'Can we go back to the beach hut?' she whispered.

Seoras nodded and, hand in hand, they walked back. Jane suggested they go into the shower because his little escapade had made her feel cold. She walked in and, without abandon, simply stripped off, turning on the water. As he followed her into the bathroom, she stood under the water expectantly, indicating he should come in with her. He stripped off too and

16

was soon holding her tight, feeling the water warming him up as well.

'Can I have a moment here?' said Jane.

'What?' said Seoras.

'Can I have a moment? We've just been dancing,' she said. 'We then went into the sea. A young couple was running in and out in the buff. We're then coming back to our wonderful pad. And now you're in the shower with me. In a shower. And yet my Seoras is miles away. My Seoras is letting the detective come out again. Letting him come to the fore and ignoring this woman in front of him.'

'Sorry,' he said. 'It's going to take time. It's just been my way, you know that. You know—'

She turned in his grip, now facing him, looking up into his eyes. 'I know,' she said, 'but you've got to let it go. You've got to let the detective retire properly. Why run and listen to those people? Who knew what they were talking about? The guy could be a joiner. He could have messed up trying to fix up somebody's kitchen or something. You act as if it's completely suspicious and you leap in. Seoras, you're not a detective anymore. You can't march in and say, "Police, here's my warrant card."'

'I know. It's the sixth sense,' said Seoras. 'Whenever I'm about, whenever I'm in places, it just goes off. Things don't feel right. You suddenly—'

Jane grabbed his buttocks with her hands. 'Does this feel right?' she said.

He grinned for a bit. 'You're trying to distract me.'

'No, I am distracting you. I told you, the detective needs to go. I want my man here.'

'The detective's part of your man too,' said Seoras.

17

'But my man needs to know when the rest of him appears, not the detective.'

Seoras simply nodded. He let the water from the shower run down in over the two of them as he held her tight.

'I think we need to go to bed,' said Jane.

'You're right, I'm exhausted.'

She smacked him on the bottom. 'Wrong, wrong! "I'm exhausted" when you're standing in the shower with the best thing in your life is not the answer.'

He gave her a grin. 'So, you're the best thing in my life, are you?'

'Damn right,' she said. 'And if you're not in that bedroom in the next minute, you won't have me in your life.'

She turned away from him, grabbing a towel and marching off to the bedroom. He smiled. Life was going to be fun with Jane. He told the detective to shut up.

Chapter 03

J ane woke up feeling invigorated. Beside her, Seoras lay asleep. She watched the rise and fall of his chest, the covers halfway down his body. They didn't do that back in Scotland, didn't leave the covers that far down. They were hauled up around you. She liked him to hold her at night, especially if she was cold, to take the chill out of her bones. But here, she'd almost been too hot through the night.

She looked across at him again and smiled. This was more like it. She'd endured too many mornings of him getting up, putting on that blessed shirt and tie, and heading out. It affected him. They all said it didn't affect them, but it did. Of course, it affected them. Heading off to investigate murders, the cases were always grim. There was no jovial murder.

Oh, I laughed when we thought about how he stabbed this one or that one. Nobody thought like that. Well, if they did, they were usually the ones Seoras was arresting. This morning, there would be no waking up and putting on a shirt and tie. When he awoke, he could stroll down to the coffeehouse. Seoras seemed happy with the coffee that was available there. That was always a good thing.

He's funny like that. Coffee this, coffee that. I'm not fussed about it, but we all have our little things. That's all he demands, and he's not a bad man for that. She rolled out of bed, walked over to the window, and went to peer through the curtains.

That was another thing. She didn't feel like throwing on a dressing gown here. She did at home. First thing she thought of. Even though they had more than adequate heating in the house at home, those early starts to the day were never truly warm, especially leaving the comfort of a bed. Here, there was no temperature change. After staring out at the rapidly brightening morning, she turned away to the shower.

As she scrubbed herself down, Jane thought about what she would do today. She'd go out this morning, get some provisions, make him breakfast, and then she might go for a walk. Jane fancied a proper hike. She wasn't sure whether he was ready for it. He was tired. There was something about retiring, and he hadn't been retired long, but he seemed to be almost recovering, winding down. She'd soon get him charging about, but he needed to switch off first. He needed to relax.

The job had him on the go—here, there, and wherever. He needed to do something that required no thought. She had challenged him with that, told him that on this holiday he needed to relax. She wouldn't hassle him. He was with her. That was more than enough. He wasn't to follow her about. She didn't want a poodle at her feet. She wanted him, Seoras.

He was a man, and he had his own things that he wanted to do. Things that would relax him. Yes, hopefully she would relax him, too. She still thought she had that about her. But beyond that, they couldn't do everything together. Not everything. They each needed something else. And he needed something that took him away, something that he didn't do anymore. Something that he could replace the police work with.

That was very much his thing. She didn't look to get involved in that. Jane had visited. She had dropped off lunch. But no, that had been his world. He needed another world now. A world to replace that one.

Jane threw on a dress and went to put a cardigan over it and then thought twice. It was bright outside. She looked at Seoras again in the bedroom, where he was still asleep. She gave a laugh, hunted down a shopping bag and then made her way out onto the dusty street.

The place was already alive, but not like last night. Last night, it had been buzzing, couples running here and there. There was love in the air. Had she just been romantic? Her head was fine. She'd had some wine. Was she feeling completely sprightly? No, but she was feeling alive. The alcohol had done nothing to stunt that.

She walked along through the market stalls and picked up some fruit. Some of it, she wasn't actually sure what it was, but it would slice and it would go on a plate. She found some bacon as well, bought some eggs and walked back along the dusty streets, stopping occasionally to look around. She saw the coffee shop and popped in. What would he want? Latte, Cortado, black or white Americano? She bought him an Americano.

It was a ridiculous name for it. She remembered growing up, and it was called a black coffee. What did they do with it now? They put it through that machine, and then they added water to it. She did not know why that was important. What was that machine? What did it do with it? Still, she'd take it back to him.

21

As she entered the house, she heard he was up; the shower running. As she entered the bedroom, he stepped out of the en-suite beyond, wrapped only in a towel.

'You sleep well, love?' she asked.

'I thought I went to bed with some woman. There was nobody here.'

'Good job,' said Jane. 'I'd have found her. I'd give her a round of the kitchens.'

He stepped forward and held her again. They kissed.

'You okay?' he said. 'You were up early.'

'I am more than okay. What are you doing today? I'm going to get breakfast.'

'Well, maybe we...'

She grabbed hold of his towel, dropped it, and strode out of the room, not once looking back. 'Don't think you can do that to me. I'm immune,' she said, walking out the door.

In her mind, she could see him shaking his head. He loved it, she knew that. She was quite feisty, and she knew that was a side of her he adored. She never quite understood how he'd been brought up. How serious he could be. But sometimes he just let it go. It did him good.

It took her about twenty minutes to make breakfast, and he arrived in a bright blue shirt with shorts on. She looked down at the socks with the sandals.

'Put the hiking boots on,' she said. 'It's quite dusty out. But if you are going to wear the sandals, don't put socks on with them.'

'Why?' asked Seoras.

'I'm the fashion guru,' said Jane. 'Although, saying that, I'm only a guru compared to you. Just go with me on these things.'

He looked at her bemused but nodded. 'I'm going to go on a

22

hike today,' she said. 'I'm going to hike over to the other side of the island and back.'

'Well, I'll come with you then.'

'No, I said I didn't want a poodle.'

Again, he looked bemused at her. 'We're here to spend time together. I'm spending time with you.'

'No, you need to switch off. What are you going to do?'

'Well,' he said, 'the guy next door called while you were out and asked if I wanted to go fishing?'

'What?' said Jane 'What guy next door?'

'He's called Shane, an Australian guy. He said he was going out on the boat. The wife didn't want to go with him. Did I want to go? I said no because I wanted to see what you were doing first.'

'Well, get back out there and tell him you're going. Go fishing. You're good to go fishing. You can fish up near Inverness, can't you?'

'I've never fished much,' said Seoras.

'You can learn then. It'll be a delightful pastime for you. Something to do that doesn't involve any brainpower. Stop that mind from thinking.'

'Are you eating the rest of that bacon?' asked Seoras.

'You have it,' she said.

After breakfast, Seoras disappeared to find Shane, and Jane made herself a small, packed lunch, throwing it in the back of a rucksack. She changed into shorts, hiking boots, and a t-shirt. Brushing her hair in front of the mirror, she gave herself a smile. She had him. He was here, and she had him. Now she was going to get fit, because the old body wasn't . . . well, he had said it was fantastic, hadn't he? Maybe he just said that, though.

Stop it, she told herself. *Look at the age of me. I am what I am. He loves it. That's enough. Don't have to be a sex symbol.* She laughed, looking in the mirror. *Was he going to run off with a younger woman? Stop for a moment. That's the thing about him. They think he's so straight, serious. When you get him alone, when you get him with you, he is a charmer.* Jane smiled again. She heard him enter through the front door.

'Have you sorted that?' she asked.

'Yes, I'm going fishing. Are you okay, though? Tell me you're okay. You're all right with my not coming with you?'

'Down, boy,' she said.

He looked at her for a moment. 'Poodle,' she said. 'I'm chasing the poodle off me.' He shook his head.

'I'll be fishing most of the day. You've got your phone on you, haven't you?'

'Yes. It works here, doesn't it?' she said.

'I was looking this morning. They've got a signal. Apparently, you get it with the accommodation. There's a limit on what you can use.'

'Well, don't be sitting surfing on it,' she said. 'It's just for getting hold of each other on different parts of the island.'

'Just be careful. Watch out for the sun. You taking a hat with you, luv?'

'I've got a hat, I'll take water with me. I've got food. Seoras, I'll be fine. There are small buses that run around the island. I don't know if you've seen them.'

'Well, I'll try to bring something back for dinner, shall I?'

'You do that,' she said. 'Don't worry about me.' She gave him a kiss and went to go, but he grabbed her hand.

'Seoras, go fish,' she said. 'Go fish because you're becoming too sentimental for my liking.'

She turned and felt him smack her on the backside. She looked back and gave him a smile. 'That's what I do,' she said.

Jane was buzzing as she exited the front door. She started off on her hike, taking in the breathtaking views of the island, but part of her was still thinking about Seoras. This was it; this was life; this was the two of them together and not so wrapped up in each other they couldn't do other things. She'd make sure they did as much as possible, saw as much as possible. Infirmity came as a shock. You didn't know from where and from when.

It was about an hour and a half later when she caught the first view of the lagoon in the middle of the island. Yes, the sea ran in towards it, but it was large. She would have to go swimming in there. Maybe she'd take him swimming in the buff like that young couple. They need to make sure nobody was about. She wouldn't want to scare people. Do it at night. She laughed. Jane felt high. High on life. She walked around the lagoon, gazing at the water, taking some photographs with her phone, and then struck out towards the far side of the island.

The guide had said previously that there was an off-limits facility but she wouldn't be going inside of that. She'd go up and around it. Close to it. Get a view of the sea beyond it.

Jane saw an aircraft coming in towards the airport but struck out more towards the cliffs near the sea, keeping away from the airport. It was a reminder that the island was busy, but here off to the side, it was quieter. She cut back in once clear of the airport and then stopped. She came across a patch of land.

There were graves marked, stones erected. She knelt in front of them, looking at the names and the dates. Of course, people must die out here too. She walked on, sweat now beginning to pour from her. It was hard work as the sun was rising, getting towards the top of the sky, and she was thankful for the enormous hat she had on. The facility was now in sight, but she cut down away from it towards the rocks, so it was practically out of view. The rocks were steep, and she looked below. There was a path cut down, well, it looked like a path. If she went down each rock, clambered down slowly, she should do it though. Would it be safe? *Oh, the hell with it,* thought Jane. *Let's get down there; let's get down and see what we can see.*

She clambered down across some rocks that were sharp, and her joints ached occasionally, but she was okay. She did nothing risky, but she felt alive as she got further down. Eventually, she found a spot. The sea was before her, crashing against the rocks. The only problem was off to the left. Part of the facility was there, and the great fence rose so you could see through it into what looked like a grey piece of concrete. A backyard of sorts.

Jane wondered what it was for. She saw some cans; that's what they looked like. Rubbish bins. Was it just a storage dump out the back? It wasn't the nicest place to look at, so she turned and looked elsewhere. You had to peer across to see the facility from where she now sat, lift your head to take a proper look. It was out of view, and she was out of view from it, so all was good. She opened up her rucksack, took out her roll, and ate. The sun was beating down, but she'd moved back into the shade.

Life was good. Life was perfect. She hadn't a clue quite what the meat inside the roll that she'd bought earlier on that day was, but she had it anyway. She'd just about finished it and thought she should head back. And she heard the first voice.

'I told you, told you quite flat, there were problems. I couldn't get it cleanly. Why can't he understand that?'

'You've disappointed him. He doesn't like to be disappointed.'

'Well, he has to be disappointed, doesn't he? What does he think people are, idiots? We take risks, you know. We take risks to get these things. And what? He just sits there.'

'Would you have disappointed him?'

Slowly, Jane turned onto her knees, pulled herself up by the rock that had sheltered her from the view of the facility at the far end of the island. She peered over now, only her eyes above the rock, not even her nose peering out. She could see two men, and they were arguing.

'You don't learn, do you?' said a voice.

One man turned away. His hands were raised. He looked annoyed, angry, but the other looked almost detached. He pulled out a gun. His arm was straight in front of him. The other man was still turned around, facing away from him, and the detached-looking man fired.

Inside Jane, her stomach flipped. She watched as the man fell forward. She collapsed backwards, the image of his head partly exploding before her eyes. Her stomach flipped again, and she fought to control it, to stop the vomit from flying out. Jane swooned, but she had the presence of mind to grab her bag. She threw what remained of the food and drinks into it, put it on her shoulders, and got herself away, away from there.

Jane didn't look back. She couldn't look back. She had to get away, get to Seoras. Seoras would know. Seoras would know what to do. Should she phone? She couldn't phone. She shouldn't phone. Jane needed to be away. If she had heard them, would they hear her?

27

She turned and looked at the cliffs in front of her. It wasn't a tough climb. It hadn't been a difficult descent. Jane had thought when she came down that she could get back up. It wouldn't be a problem. But now it seemed like a struggle. Her feet didn't find the same places. She scrambled, and this foot slipped, and then that foot went, and then she pulled herself upwards again.

It felt like an hour getting back up the cliff, but maybe it was only five minutes. *That gun rising, the arm straight.* She got to the top; the ground seemed to roll this way and that. She thought she would be sick again, and then she stumbled on. Stumbled towards the lagoon. The lagoon was back that way. That's where she would need to go. That way, and from the lagoon, she would get to Seoras.

Sweat poured off her, and yet she felt chilled, deeply chilled. What was it? Was this just heatstroke, though? What was going on? No, she had seen someone. She had seen that man. He'd died. He'd been shot. They'd shot him. Seoras, they'd shot him!

Jane walked, but she saw no one. Where was everyone? Where on earth was she? The lagoon? Was the lagoon over there? Was it? She stumbled now, walking on and on. And then she felt herself pitch forward. She felt herself hit the ground. And then she felt nothing.

Chapter 04

Her head pounded. That was the first thing she noticed. Her eyes hadn't opened yet, but Jane heard him. And she felt a hand running across the top of her head, fingers going through her hair in a way only Seoras did. She mouthed the word 'Seoras.'

'I'm here.' His tone was caring, but it was worried. 'Take it easy. Just take it easy.'

'Seoras, where—'

'You're safe,' he said. 'You're perfectly safe. I'm here. You're in the medical facility. They found you, but you're safe. Take it easy.'

Slowly her eyes opened, and at first, they were blurry. There was a bright light, but she was cool. *Air conditioning,* she thought. *That's air conditioning. It's that type of cool. You didn't find that type of coolness naturally here.* The beach hut didn't have air conditioning. She didn't want air conditioning, but here in the hospital, maybe they had to, maybe that was important.

Her eyes focused. The first thing she saw was Seoras's fedora hat. It was sitting on the table beside the bed. She turned her head and looked up into his face. Worry was all over it. He wasn't good at hiding worry. When he was bothered, he was bothered. The man had a brain that could delve into some of the darkest minds. He could see motive from miles off but he didn't have a poker face.

'You're okay. They're putting fluids into you. You got dehydrated. Got into trouble. They found you. A couple of holidaymakers spotted you and raised the alarm. They got you here. They got me out on the boat. Found me and brought me back. They said you'll be fine. You just need to hydrate again. Need a bit of rest.'

'Are we alone?' she said.

'We're in the medical centre,' said Seoras. 'The doctor's here and the nurses are about. I wouldn't say we're alone. Besides, you need to get better.'

Jane felt her stomach roll. She'd seen something, hadn't she? She'd seen . . . had she? Had she seen someone get shot? Or had it been dehydration? Had she fantasised about that? Had that just been something in her mind? Her life, talking to Seoras, had been all about people who'd been killed. Intrigue and mystery, but she'd seen this one, hadn't she?

'Where did they find me?'

'Near to the lagoon,' said Seoras. 'Where'd you been?'

'I'm not sure,' said Jane. 'I thought I went all the way over the island, maybe near the facility. Stumbled back, but I don't know now. Things seem a blur. I thought I had gone and had lunch.'

'You'd eaten your lunch,' said Seoras. 'I checked. I got your bag. You hadn't drunk enough water though, I don't think.'

The nurse at the back of the room approached the bed. Jane hadn't spotted her before, but the dark-skinned woman smiled at her.

'Overdone it,' she said. 'You'll be fine. You'll be okay. Rest, get fluids into you and feel better, and there's no better place to rest than this. The doctor will say when you can come out of here, but it shouldn't be long, once we know that you're on the mend.'

Jane's hand went forward and grabbed Seoras's. 'I don't remember it well,' she said.

'It's fine. You don't have to.' The door opened behind him; a doctor in a white coat walked in. He was a youngish man, fairly attractive, his hair swept back across his head. He grinned at her.

'A little too much today, was it?' he said.

'Maybe.'

'Where did you go?' asked the doctor.

'Walked across the island.'

'Do you remember where?'

'I remember the lagoon,' said Jane. She was about to say the facility and then she stopped herself. *Should I tell him what she saw? No, I'm just probably nuts*, she thought. *Probably just a figment of my imagination. I might tell Seoras.* The vision of the man came back to her. The outstretched arm. The arm was so solid. Unwavering. *If you were shooting someone, you'd be nervous, surely. Ending someone's life. Just like that. Out the back. Taken out the back and disposed of. Like a mouse. Like a mouse caught in the trap.* She felt herself shiver.

'We're going to have to take it easy,' said the doctor. 'I think we might keep you for a little while. Then you can get back to the accommodation, but again, taking it easy.'

'Okay,' said Jane. She closed her eyes again and heard the doctor say, 'You need to be very careful. Very dangerous out here if you're not used to this sort of sun.'

31

'Oh, we live in Scotland,' said Seoras. 'I don't think we've seen the sun.'

She squeezed his hand and felt his other hand running through her hair again. Seoras was here. It would be okay.

Jane drifted off. The next time she came around, she saw he was there again, sitting by her bed.

'Have you not gone and got something to eat?'

'You don't have to be worried about me, woman,' said Seoras. 'You're the one in trouble here. You're the one who needs help. I'm perfectly capable of getting myself something to eat.'

'I'm sorry,' she said. 'Sorry.'

'Don't be sorry. Just be what they say and get better. Yes?'

A nurse came up from behind Seoras. And knelt down beside her. 'You had a rough time,' she said. 'Are you feeling any better?'

'I think so,' Jane said.

'The lagoon's quite something, isn't it?' said the nurse.

'Yes, yes, it was, and . . .'

'And what?' asked the nurse. 'What else did you see when you were out there?'

'You have a graveyard,' she said. 'Stones, round stones.'

'Oh right, you went there. That's beyond the lagoon. It sits in the middle of the island, doesn't it?'

'Where's that?' she heard Seoras ask.

'You go to the lagoon, round the lagoon,' said Jane, 'and then you can either take one side of the lagoon or the other. Little island community. I guess people must die at times.'

'Well, sometimes people get out of their depth,' said the nurse. 'Sometimes people make a mistake. You know? We had a guy fall off a jet ski once. Couldn't save him. Terrible shame, but they buried him here.'

'How many people live here permanently?' asked Seoras.

'I don't know. A couple of hundred,' said the nurse.

Then Jane slipped away again. She was exhausted, but her mind was spinning again, seeing that image once more.

It was the sound of the door that woke her up. She was sure of it. It almost thudded, and then there were feet coming to attention. It just felt like an urgency in the room, except for the hand that was holding hers. She opened her eyes to see Seoras again, but his head was turned. He was looking at a man.

The man was small but dressed impeccably. He had a white suit on, the white shirt underneath. On his head was a Panama hat. There was a red handkerchief in the pocket of his suit jacket, and he was walking across to her bedside, on the opposite side from where Seoras sat.

'Forgive me. I must introduce myself. My name is Wainwright, and this is my island. I was shocked to hear about what happened to you, so I wanted to come personally just to make sure you're all right. We do try to look after our guests.'

'Your medical attention has been excellent,' said Seoras. 'I'm Seoras Macleod; this is Jane, my partner.'

Jane saw Seoras put his hand over. Guy Montag shook it, but then he turned back to Jane.

'A little too much hiking, the tropical sun catches out people. I've been thinking about it; we really need to put some sort of shelters up. Whereabouts were you? I guess. Somebody said you were possibly by the lagoon. The lagoon would be good for a bit more shelter, wouldn't it? People like to go to the lagoon. Have you been there?' He said, turning around to Seoras.

'No, we've just arrived. Only yesterday.'

'And you were off hiking,' Wainwright said to Jane. She managed to nod.

'Hiking's not something I think about with people on the island. You look at the jet skis or the fishing or swimming in the lagoon. Or some people race around on buggies. Things like that, you know. Or they like the bit of nightlife we have. People playing cards late at night. Dancing, music.'

'We were at one of your restaurants,' said Seoras. 'There aren't that many, are there?'

'No, no, but they are good, aren't they?'

'Yes, yes,' says Seoras. 'We enjoyed it. The food was excellent, and we were dancing too. I hope that hasn't taken it out of her.'

'I can dance,' said Jane, almost in a whisper. 'Was just hiking. I think it's the sun.'

'You got up to the lagoon,' said Wainwright. 'Where did you go after that? Somebody said the graveyard.'

'I did. I got to the graveyard.'

'Were you making for there? Was that your intention?'

'No, no,' she said.

'Morbid to head for a graveyard,' said Seoras.

'That's what I was thinking,' said the island owner. 'But I'm thinking about shelters and places out of the sun. I mean, if I had put a shelter there, you could have just gone underneath it if you'd felt bad. Where did you go after that?'

'I don't know,' said Jane. 'Stumbled about. I guess I must have been overcome. I ate my lunch at some point.'

'Didn't have enough water with you. Must have taken it out of you. Forgive me for asking, but are you prone to difficulties like this? If you have medical conditions, please tell our doctor so he can understand. There's nothing else going on behind this? If there is a need for us to get you somewhere else, we will fly you there. I mean, I want to look after you. I want to make sure you're okay. Am I being too forward? Sometimes I, well . . . I'm sorry, I'm just used to running my own businesses and companies and things, and I just ask the questions. This is, of course, your private medical issue. I don't wish to pry, but if there is something, we can provide the transport. It won't cost anything. Don't worry about medical insurance and stuff like that. We'll get you somewhere. We'll look after you.'

'Thank you,' said Seoras. 'I think she's just dehydrated. That's what the doctor said. Jane has nothing underlying that I would be worried about.'

Jane lifted her head, shook it and said, 'No, nothing.'

'Well, if you think of anything,' said Wainwright, 'if you think of where you were, please let me know because I want to think about seriously putting up shelters.'

'Well, you said that the facility is off-limits, and I understand that,' said Seoras, 'but I don't think Jane was too far up that way. I would suspect not.'

'Well, there's nothing wrong, of course,' said Wainwright, 'as long as you don't enter the facility, and that's as much for your own protection. It's a workplace. It's a factory of sorts. There are dangers within there you wouldn't know about unless you work there and you're briefed. So, please just be careful if you go near it. Don't go inside.'

'You have plenty of security about anyway,' said Soros. 'I'm sure they would spot any of us who absentmindedly made their way in. It's the fences that I saw when we flew in. I wouldn't have believed it to be possible to stumble in.'

'Well, we do our best,' said Wainwright. 'Where are you from?'

35

'Scotland.'

'And retired, are you? Sorry,' Wainwright said. 'That's presumptuous, isn't it? I didn't mean you look old or anything. That's terrible. I really must talk with a bit more thought.'

'I am retired, as a matter of fact. I'm a former detective chief inspector,' said Seoras.

'And your lovely wife?'

'Partner. Jane's my partner,' said Seoras. 'It's been a while since she worked. She moved up to be with me. Former traffic warden.'

'Oh, I don't want to cross you then,' said Wainwright.

'I'll give you a ticket,' said Jane dryly. The man laughed almost too much.

'Well, you have a think about what I said. And if you know where you were, please tell us. Any of us here. The rest of them know how to find me. I'm going to pop in on you later in the week. But I hope you get back on your feet and enjoy yourself. Please enjoy yourself. If there's anything here that's not up to speed or you need something or help, do contact us. Tell them Mr Wainwright said get in touch with him.'

'Well, that's awfully decent of you,' said Seoras. 'Very kind, but I think she'll be all right. Your excellent medical facility is taking care of things.'

'Excellent,' said Wainwright. 'That's excellent.' He went to leave, got to the door and turned around again. 'Like I say, anything comes to mind about where you were or whatever, let me know.' He disappeared.

Jane lay as Seoras sat, saying nothing. He propped her up eventually, using a couple of pillows and with the help of the nurse, and she could look across the room properly. There was a TV on, playing a film.

'What time is it?' Jane said.

'It's midnight,' said Seoras.

'Midnight? Go, go to bed,' she said.

'I don't think they allow you to have fancy men in with you.'

She pushed an arm at him, but she was tired, far too weak. 'I'll be fine,' she said. 'Go.'

Seoras got up and kissed her. 'I'll be back first thing in the morning,' he said.

'No, don't,' she said. 'Rest up. I am perfectly fine. Did the doctor say I was in any danger?'

'No,' said Seoras. 'He said that you'd be here overnight. They just wanted to watch you. But all signs are good.'

'Well then, clear off,' she said.

'You going to be okay?'

'I don't know if I'll sleep. But there's something on.'

'There are lots of films over there. You want me to put a DVD in?' asked Seoras. 'I'll sit here and watch it with you.'

'Would you just go?' she said. He nodded and went to go to the door.

'Where are you going?' Jane asked.

'Are you all right?'

'I said, "Where are you going?" I'm fine.'

He looked confused. She raised her hand, and with her finger beckoned him to come back over. He did so, and as he got close, she put her hand up on his cheek. And then gently pulled him towards her. She kissed him deeply and then when she let go, she said, 'I'm fine. You must have worn me out the night before.'

It suddenly dawned on him what she meant, that she needed her kiss before he would leave.

'Well, if I'm too much for you . . .'

She lightly slapped him on the cheek. 'When I get out of here, I'm going to put you back in this bed.'

'Promises,' he said.

'Well, if you're going to settle for a cuddle, it'll have to be that,' she said. Jane smiled, kissed him again, and watched as he left. She looked over at the screen. *Gone with the Wind, isn't it?*

Jane closed her eyes, sitting upright. She'd been drifting so much in her sleep. She wasn't ready to go back. Instead, she tried to think about what she would do for the rest of the holiday, but there was the facility again. Had she been to the facility? Had she seen the place out the back? Her stomach turned within her. She felt her hands gripping the bedsheets. 'You need to relax,' she said. She eased herself down the bed until she was almost horizontal and waited, desperately thinking about nothing until she fell asleep.

Chapter 05

I n the late afternoon, Jane was getting sick of it. Several of the staff had come up to her and asked the same question. Where had she been? Where had she gone? Some said that Mr Wainwright wanted to know to put up his shelters, and they were keen that they could tell him, describing it as being able to get one up in their job. But it was relentless.

Seoras had come back in the morning, but she'd sent him off, because all she would do was lie there, resting up. They'd said that she was probably ready to leave that evening. She would have felt much more refreshed except for the constant questions from the nursing staff and doctors. She thought she'd had three different doctors look in on her, for a case of what? Heat stroke? It seemed insane. Or maybe they were just looking after their guest, not wanting it to get out that a guest had suffered. Still, she thought it strange.

By the time Seoras had arrived back in the evening, she was already dressed and ready to go. She thanked the doctors and the nurses for their care but was keen to get out of there quickly, taking Seoras's arm and then a taxi back to their accommodation. She could see him watching her.

He cooked some fish that he had caught while out on that

fateful day and she ate it, with no wine, just to be safe. Then Jane settled down in a chair just outside the accommodation. Seoras disappeared to buy coffee at the coffee shop, came back and sat down beside her, saying very little. She nodded off once or twice while watching the waves. Slowly the sun set, the fire descending and being eaten up by the water, before the moon, on a cloudless night, lit up the bay.

Jane said that they should go down to the water again, sit out on the beach closer to it. Seoras picked up a lounger and carried it all the way down, offering it to Jane. She tapped it, showing Seoras should lie down first. And then she lay beside him on it, taking his arms and placing them around her.

'You okay?' he whispered.

'Getting there, I think.'

'It takes longer to get over it these days.'

'Stop,' she said. 'We will not talk about being older. Older is not a word we're going to use.'

'Mature,' he blurted.

She dug her elbow into his ribs.

'Seasoned.' Another dig in the ribs.

It was getting close to midnight as they lay there. But Jane did not feel at all sleepy now. She wondered if Seoras did, as he wasn't moving. Neither was he snoring. Every now and then, she'd feel her hair being tousled. He liked that. It was a thing of his, but it meant he was awake.

As they lay there, looking up at the moon, two figures raced past them. A couple of bare buttocks entered the water, and Jane could hear Seoras give a little laugh.

'What?' she said.

'They're out here again.'

'They're only young and having fun,' she said.

'I think that's why you wanted to come here. You wanted to see him hit the water.'

'I'd rather see you,' she said.

'That's not going to wash,' said Seoras. 'There's a lot of things I'll take, but that's really not true, is it?'

She started to laugh. The young couple raced past them again, heading back to their beach hut. Seoras quietly said, 'They're not very shy, are they?' Jane found herself laughing. But then she went quiet, as if something inside said, 'You can't laugh at a time like this.'

'What's wrong?' he asked.

She turned over. She was still cuddling Seoras, but now faced him. 'I think I saw something before I collapsed.'

'You think you saw something? What?'

'I went up to the facility. Never told them that. I told them everything short of it because of what I saw.'

'Go on,' said Seoras. His face was full of concern, but it wasn't angry. It was inquisitive, though.

'I went up towards the facility, but I deliberately headed away from it, down to the coast, and went down the cliffs. As I got to the bottom, I found a little perch that I could look out to the sea from. I couldn't see the facility from there, although it was just over, not far away. If I stood up, I could see it. Well, at least the back end of it, like a concrete plinth area at the back. It had a fence around it, but nobody was there. Eating my lunch, I heard two voices, two people talking. There was some sort of disappointment. I can't remember exactly, and then I heard them arguing. I looked because I heard them arguing. Peered up over the rock, and I saw one man. He had his arm extended straight out and had a gun in it.'

'A gun?' said Seoras. 'Are you sure it was a gun?'

41

Jane shivered. 'Yes,' she said, 'because he pulled the trigger. The other man was facing away from him. It blew the back of his head off.'

She went quiet. Seoras pulled her to him, and she took his embrace for a while. But then she gently pushed back and looked up at him. 'I have told no one. I didn't think I should tell anyone. I thought—'

He put a finger up to her lips. 'Let's take it from the top. You were down on the rocks. You had gone down the rocks. Yes.'

'Yes,' she said.

'Would you be able to find that place again?' She nodded. 'Would you describe them for me? How did you get down to them?'

'I told you,' she said. 'I climbed down the rocks.'

'No,' he said. 'Describe it. Describe what the climb was like. Every bit of it.'

'Why? It's hardly important, is it?' she said. 'I just told you what the bad bit was.'

'Easy,' said Seoras. 'Quietly. Bedroom voices,' he said.

Jane nodded, realising they were out in the public, and if anyone overheard what she was saying, well, who knew how they would take it.

'At first, I went down forward facing. There were a couple of places where I had to turn, and I had to put my feet down as I held on with my hands. But not that difficult a descent because I wouldn't have tried it otherwise. I wasn't being reckless, stupid.'

'And when you got there, describe the place you were sitting.'

'Well,' said Jane, 'on my left, there was like a wall of rock. If I stood up, I could just about see over the top of it. My nose wouldn't have cleared it, though. Looking out, there were more rocks dropping off the front, but they were too dangerous to go near. And then it was a drop to the sea.'

'Tell me about the sea.'

'The sea. It was that blue, a deep—no, it wasn't,' she said suddenly. 'It was almost green, that sort of light green colour, where the sands come up quite close underneath it. That's what it was at first, and then when you went further out, it got to a deeper blue.'

'And the waves?'

'There were waves breaking down at the rocks, but I couldn't see them from where I was sitting. I'd seen them on the way down, though, further along, but the waves out there, they weren't breaking. They were just moseying up and down. Quite beautiful.'

'Tell me about the plinth. Tell me about the back of the facility.'

'I said it was like a plinth. It was like a big concrete plinth. Big, though, enormous, not like the patio at the back of our house. Maybe about four or five patios, and I couldn't see to the left. There was a building that ended, and there was this plinth area, fencing around it, but the fencing was crosshatch; it didn't obscure what you could see.'

'Would someone see it from the water?' asked Seoras.

'Yes, yes, you would.'

He nodded. 'Would you have seen it from the top of the rocks?'

'Not from where I climbed down from, I guess if you went a lot closer to the facility you'd eventually see it.'

'Could you see the facility from where you climbed down?'

'At the top,' said Jane, 'not really. You could see the tops of the fence.'

43

Again, he nodded. 'Describe to me once again what happened between the two men.'

'The first one was at one end of the plinth. He was looking back at the other . And they were arguing. Arguing about something. Someone hadn't done something right for someone. And they would be annoyed. They'd be unhappy. Something like that. And then one of them, he turned away in disgust after berating the other one. Then the other one pulled the gun. It was held with a very straight arm.'

'Any bend in the arm?' asked Seoras.

'It was so straight, it was… No, yes, yes there was, very slight.'

'And the man fired,' said Seoras.

'And the other man toppled forward, but it was like something blew off the back of his head, like out the front.'

'Was there a sound?' asked Seoras.

'None,' she said.

'What about the gun? Did it have a long barrel at all?'

'It looked long. I couldn't see it that well. I assumed it was a gun because it was in his hand and it had a point out the front, and it fired a bullet, so it was a gun to me. Seoras, I couldn't have identified it.'

He pulled her close, and she lay with her head on his chest. He didn't say anything. But every now and again he would pull her tighter.

'What are you thinking?'

'I'm thinking,' Seoras said.

'But am I telling the truth? Am I?'

'I'm thinking.'

She turned away from him, her back to him, but he pulled her tight again. His hand ruffled through her hair. He was thinking. This was the thing about Seoras. He didn't just blurt out the first thing. Anything important ran around in there. It got chewed over. It was tossed about like some sort of giant compactor machine and eventually it would squeeze out, distilled to the purest solution. She had told him to leave the detective behind, and here she was handing him a case, handing him a potential murder.

'Have you told anybody else?' he whispered.

'No one. I didn't tell anybody I was up near the facility either . . . and they asked. They asked constantly. They asked me all the time where I'd gone when I had this heat stroke. Do you think it could be the heat stroke that's caused it, though? Was I seeing things? Was I . . .'

'Listen,' he said in her ear. 'You have described to me getting down the rocks, described to me what you saw. You've described it to me more than once, and it all fits and tallies. What I believe is that you think you saw it. Now, whether that's caused by the heat stroke, whether or not it's real, I don't know. I haven't got enough evidence to make a dispassionate judgment on that.'

'So, what do we do?'

'The first thing we do is we don't tell anyone. If you tell them, and you have actually seen a killing, we're in trouble. Where do we go? If, however, you've made it up, you're going to cause trouble.'

'Okay,' said Jane. 'I can keep quiet, but what do we do? We can't just let it slide, can we?'

'No,' said Seoras. 'What we'll do is we'll go there. Take you back to where you saw something. It might cause you to remember things. It might enable me to work out whether you imagined it or not.'

'So what? We walk there tomorrow?'

'We don't walk there. Worst-case scenario,' said Seoras, 'what if you actually did see a killing. If you did, and if we walk out there, well then, they'll know we're coming back to think about it, to look at it. They're not sure what you saw at the moment, and we want to keep it that way. We'll take a boat. After all, that's reasonable. I was off fishing. You are walking, but you've had heatstroke, so I'm bringing you on the boat with me this time. Somewhere you can shelter, and you're safe, and I'm with you. That will look reasonable. But we'll go round by there, so we'll have good reason to go. We'll look for certain types of fish or whatever. I'll make it work.'

'Seoras,' she said, 'do you think I'm going nuts?'

'You've either had a tremendous fright, or you've had heatstroke,' he said calmly. 'Either way, we need to work out what happened. We need to work out whether it was real or not. If it isn't, you just drink plenty of water and get better. If it is . . .'

'What if it is?' asked Jane.

'Well, then we might have to bring the detective back, and we'll have to watch our step because there'll be killers on the loose.'

Chapter 06

Seoras Macleod was up early that morning. At six o'clock he was out of bed, turning to see Jane still lying there, deep in sleep. He let her rest and left her a note saying he was off to organise a fishing trip. Seoras moseyed his way along to the coffee shop, which opened early, and asked inside about good people to recommend where to fish, and who to hire a boat from. He was told that in about an hour's time he could try over by the docks.

Seoras sat with his coffee, but inside he was twitchy. He didn't know what to think about what Jane said. The obvious deductions were if she was wrong, she had just suffered from heatstroke. It was important for her to know that though, because to her it had looked incredibly real. If it were real, well then, he was on an island far, far away wondering how to deal with this. He wasn't even sure he had any type of jurisdiction.

When he wandered down to the docks, Seoras could see boats for hire and grabbed hold of one man. He was sitting clearly feeling a little rough from the night before. His boat wasn't that big but adequate. Seoras also needed a reason to go around to that side of the island.

'I want to do some fishing. How much is the boat to hire?'

'How long do you want it for?'

'Take it today. I'll have it back before dinnertime.'

The man showed a number, and Seoras passed over several notes.

'Can you give me a little bit of help with what's out and about on the island? What's good to catch and where?'

The man railed on about different fish, where they would be caught, and whether he'd have to go far from the shore. He also said there were crabs on the far side, but not to go too close to the facility. Some of the guards didn't like that, but it was excellent for crabbing.

'Brilliant. My partner, she loves crab. That would be a perfect choice,' said Seoras.

The man showed the crab lines within the boat, and Seoras made his way back to the beach hut, where Jane had arisen. She looked gaunt as she stood there, frying bacon in a pan.

'You need to freshen up a bit,' he said.

'I've gone through a rough time.'

'And you need to be someone who's coming out of that and looking okay. Yes?'

'But I'm not okay. I still don't know what I saw.'

'But they don't know that. They think you've had heatstroke, and we want them to think that you're just recovering from it and you're fine. Show them you're not dwelling on other things because if they think you are and the other things are real, we could be in trouble.'

'And that's meant to make me feel better?'

'No, it's meant to give you a little boost to get yourself sorted,' he said. Seoras came up to her and put his arms around her. 'You've got to go out today and you're going to do some sunbathing, though you don't want to, but you need to do some on the boat so anybody sailing by thinks you're fine.'

'Okay,' she said.

Jane tipped out the bacon onto a plate and did some toast with it, which the two of them ate. Then she disappeared off to the shower while Seoras sat inside the beach hut pondering what had gone on. When she came out dressed in a long sarong and a bikini top, she gave him a smile. *She's done well*, he thought. To most people she looked like Jane, excited, bubbly, lively, but Seoras could see through it. He could see the pain underneath, the wonder at what had gone on.

'Good,' he said. 'You look great as ever.'

'I'll try my best,' she said. Jane took his hand, and he led her out into the town, where they picked up a couple of pre-made sandwiches, fruit, and drinks, taking them on board the boat. The day was hot and sunny, but Jane brought a floppy hat, while Seoras was wearing his fedora. He had this habit now of lifting it up with his hand, briefly, to say goodbye to people, or to acknowledge them, instead of just using his hand to wave. He looked almost jaunty as they pulled out of the docks, but inside, he was completely focused.

The boat made way around the side of the island, and Jane pointed at some cliffs that she'd passed on her walk. There was an entrance towards the lagoon on the other side, but on this side, the land narrowed before heading round and further north up to the facility. At one stage, Jane stopped and pointed up to the land.

'In the middle of there,' she said, 'that's what the graveyard is. I definitely saw that. I saw it over there. I'm not sure about the way back.'

'Don't force it,' said Seoras. 'Just let it come. Tell me what

49

you see in your mind, but don't force it. Don't push something in that isn't there.'

'What? The graveyard is there. You can look at it if you want.'

'Not sure there's a point to that.'

He steered the boat out towards the facility and soon was sitting a fair distance off land, looking back in. There was a pair of binoculars on the boat, and he picked them up and could soon spy the plinth that had been described by Jane. The concrete patch at the rear of the facility was indeed guarded by a high fence. It was criss-cross hatched and see-through.

'What do you see?' asked Jane.

'Well, there's nothing to dispute in what you say you saw so far. The surrounding fence, you can see through. Given I have binoculars, you would have been a lot closer. And it's certainly at the rear, away from everybody. There aren't very many boats out here either. However, I think it must have been a silenced weapon if it's been used. The noise would ricochet off the rocks, and everyone would hear it. A gun retort is loud. Louder than most people think. But you wouldn't even notice a silenced weapon. Not with a sea on the move and the odd crash of waves.'

'Is this where we have to stay, then?' she asked.

'No, we'll go closer. I didn't want to be standing staring from so close with binoculars. Makes you look like you're looking at them. We just want to be there, naturally. That's who we need to be portraying. The facility's just there. We're doing what we're doing.'

'Which is?' she asked.

'We're going crabbing.' He pushed the throttle down on the boat and soon they were resting offshore, anchored over the top of what was advised as good crabbing ground. He baited some lines and dropped them over the side, telling Jane to hold one. As he did so, Seoras looked up.

'Over there on the rocks, you came down from the top. How far back?'

'Must have been a good two hundred metres, and it curved down before coming to that plateau there, that area. Can you see it?' asked Jane.

Seoras nodded. He stared along the line of the rocks. She certainly could have climbed down them. He wouldn't have had a problem. He felt a pull on one of his lines. Pulling it up, he took the crab off, placed it in a bucket.

'Certainly, seemed to have a line of sight,' he told her. 'So, it's perfectly reasonable that you could have got there and had a look.'

'But did I?' asked Jane.

'That's difficult to say. If I could get up to that plinth, we might have a look and see if there were any remains, any blood or stains. But I haven't got a forensic team with me. And besides, they would clear up. I mean, they wouldn't leave a body just lying there. It's a facility. So, somebody would clean up. Nobody has said anything about it, though.'

'But maybe the people from the facility killed him. Maybe that's what they haven't said.'

'Or maybe it was two people having a row, and the killer wants to make sure that it doesn't go anywhere else,' said Seoras. 'You can't jump to conclusions.'

'So, what do we do? Now we're here,' she said.

'Well, the first thing we do is catch more crabs,' said Seoras. 'That's why we're here, so we have to do that.'

'We could ask the doctor if it really was heatstroke. If he

found anything to confirm it.'

'Well, you had heat exhaustion of some sort because you were lying there. Now, if that trauma was caused by this, and you ended up stumbling blindly and then succumbed to the heat, I don't think he's going to tell the difference. But I also don't want to ask him.'

'Why not?' asked Jane.

'Because if he works for the governor, well then, and the governor's somehow tied into this, we would be in trouble.'

'They asked me constantly. Asked me where I'd gone, what I'd been doing.'

'I noted that last night, the number of people that kept asking. Desperate to know to put up shelters. Why would you be so desperate to know to put up shelter?' said Seoras. 'You just put it up. I mean, somebody's bound to use it at some point. You don't need to go desperately asking and questioning people. Especially harassing them after they've had heatstroke,' said Seoras. 'You would think you would have just put some plans in place, anyway. Funny.'

Seoras could hear a boat coming and looked around him. There was a small rubber dinghy coming towards them with two guards on board. One of them had a gun, and Seoras gave him a wave as he sped towards the boat.

'Hello,' said Seoras. 'What's the matter? Something we can help with?'

'Oh, good day to you, sir. I'm just out here wondering what you're doing.'

'Crabbing. I went down to the harbour to do some fishing, and they said it was good crabbing here. So, I thought, well, we'll do that. My wife here had heatstroke yesterday, so I want to keep her close. You can understand that, can't you?'

'Oh absolutely,' said the man. 'And this is the only place you've been?'

'No, we came round the island for a bit of a view and then we came over here. Like I said, we've got all the crabbing gear here. We've caught some. Hopefully, we can cook them up tonight.'

The man stared at him for a moment and then Seoras pulled up one of the lines with a crab on it. He picked it up and put the crab in a bucket.

'We have to come out, sir,' said the guard. 'There's somebody on a boat sitting watching the facility, so we check who they are.'

'Oh, we're staying—maybe you know—on the other side of the island.'

'Very good. Some people take pictures of the facility and that. I would advise you not to because it causes more hassle. They like their privacy because of what we produce within. We're specialists, you see. You can't get much of it anywhere else. We just want to make sure that nobody gets a lot of the secrets that the company holds. That's the thing about pharmaceuticals and the like, sir.'

'Oh, I understand,' said Seoras. 'Don't worry, we're not taking any photographs. Not interested in what your guards are doing. Just want my crab and then we'll head back later.'

'And how is your good lady?' the man asked.

'She's doing okay. She's still under the weather. That's the trouble with dehydration. It knocks it out of you. You can only put it back slowly, bit by bit, but hey, she's doing okay.'

'Very good,' said the man. 'I'll leave you in peace. Just wanted to check.' They watched the boat disappear, its wake spreading behind it.

'Well, we've seen everything,' said Jane. 'Shall we go?'

'No,' said Seoras. 'That would tell them we're running off because we're worried we're going to get caught doing something. We're not. We're here crabbing, and we will crab for the rest of the day.'

'But we need to look into things,' said Jane. 'We need to work out—'

'Easy, Sherlock,' said Seoras. 'Come over here a minute.'

She stood up in her sarong and walked over to him. He put his arms around her and kissed her, held her tight before turning her around so that she was facing the crabbing lines.

'One on the left. Pick it up. Pull it up. There'll be a crab on it,' he said. She did so and then he helped her reach in with her hands to get in behind the pincers before throwing the crab into a bucket.

'Why did you get me to do that?' she said.

'We're out here fishing. You're the only companion with me. I'm teaching you to fish. Teaching you how to go crabbing. It's important. It makes them think that we're here doing something other than looking at them.'

'Do you think I'm mad though?' asked Jane. 'You've looked at it now. You've seen the guards come out.'

'I don't think you're mad, but we still got a problem.'

'What's that?' asked Jane.

'If you saw something genuine, the only way to prove it is to have a body. If there's no body, we'll not prove it. I wouldn't be offering anything until I am happy I can prove it because if it happened over there, somebody in that facility is part and parcel of the murder. I've had enough experience to know that when people cover up a murder, they don't mess about. Where do we go here? We're on an island. We're miles away.

The only airplanes out are coming from their airport. It's not easy. We're on our own. I've been on my own before,' he said. 'And this time I've got you.'

'What use am I going to be to you?'

'Hopefully a bit more than moral inspiration,' he said. 'We need to find a body. If we say somebody's dead, we need to show them. And show them they're not living, not simply disappeared. It's difficult without a body.'

They spent the rest of the day crabbing until there was a full bucket. Seoras made his way back in the boat, Jane lying out in the sun on deck. They handed the boat back and together, walking hand in hand, they carried the bucket of crabs back. When they got inside, Seoras turned to Jane.

'So are we going to have crab tonight?' he said.

'Do you know how to cook it?' asked Jane.

Seoras looked at her. 'No. I thought you would.'

'We could dress it or that,' she said.

'I don't know how. We need to use them up though.'

'Let me,' she said.

An hour and a half later, he was sitting at the restaurant, plates of crab, dressed and prepared, before them. Several other customers were having crab as well, and Jane was sitting with some notes, wrapped up in a little roll.

'They pay well for the seafood here,' she said. Seoras grinned. She was certainly resourceful if nothing else, but a part of him was anxious. He had no backup to go to here, and he was scared he was going to need it.

Chapter 07

Seoras and Jane were heading back from the restaurant. The evening was still warm, but a wind had picked up. Jane had her arm wrapped through Seoras' and the two strolled gently along the dusty road back towards their accommodation. As they did so, they could see a woman coming towards them. She had long black hair that seemed to sway around her bare shoulders. A strapless top led to a wavy skirt underneath, which was cut up on one side, revealing most of one leg. She was maybe thirty at most, possibly younger. And while she definitely caught Seoras's eye at first, he paid her no attention as he walked along with Jane.

They weren't speaking to each other, just happy to be in each other's company as they returned to their accommodation. There were other things running through his mind, thoughts about what Jane had seen. The reactions they'd had on the island. The push for seeing what she knew. In Seoras's head, the murder was real, and people were reacting to Jane to see what she had seen.

They must not have understood she was actually there, had actually witnessed it. If they had thought that, they would have hunted her down quickly. It was a game of cat and mouse to see what she knew; the tourist found close to the deed.

As they walked along, Seoras was surprised to see that the woman had crossed over the street and was now making a beeline for him. He could feel Jane pulling tighter on his arm, almost as if clutching him to her, to say 'mine.'

'Excuse me,' said the woman.

'Hello,' said Seoras. 'Can I help?'

'You wouldn't have the time on you, would you?'

The woman wore no wristwatch, not an uncommon feature amongst younger people today, and Seoras turned to his to look. 'Almost eleven,' he said.

'Thank you,' said the woman. 'I don't suppose you'd like to come for a drink? I'm meeting someone at midnight but, to be honest, I'd rather be sitting with a crowd. You look like a man who could protect a woman.'

'I'm afraid we're on our own. We'd rather get back.'

Seoras almost started at Jane's response. It was a quick brush-off.

'I really could do with some help,' said the woman. Her arm was now stroking Seoras's forearm, making him almost blush. He looked at the woman. She was now staring into his eyes. She gave a smile, and he thought he was in an advert. That's what they did in TV adverts, wasn't it? The attractive woman.

He remembered the one where you never saw the man; you just saw the woman holding her hand out, dragging him here and there. And the woman was attractive, and the woman was friendly, and never struggled with something in her eye, or was caught unaware by a bout of sneezing. He almost laughed internally, but he was wary of who he was looking at.

'It'd only be an hour. Would you please?' The woman looked at Seoras, never at Jane, and was almost tugging on his arm.

He felt Jane tug the other way.

'I'm afraid we can't. Not at all,' said Jane. 'I'm sorry, we need to get back.'

'I'll buy you your drinks; it's not a problem,' said the woman. 'Maybe you could come.'

'We're out together,' said Jane. 'We need to spend some time together. I'm sorry, but we need to—'

'We don't really,' said Seoras. He felt his arm being squeezed tighter by Jane.

'I think we do. I think it is something we have to do.'

'The lady needs protection,' said Seoras, glancing at Jane, then back to the woman. He let his eyes drift up and down her.

'Oh, would you? Please?'

'No, we won't,' said Jane. 'We need to get back. We've got certain things we need to discuss. We're out here together. I'm afraid not. Just go up to the bar. Go and sit up by the bar. I'm sure the bartender will look after you for an hour. They seem pretty nice in there. Or go and sit in one of the restaurants.'

'I'm sure we can spare an hour for the poor woman,' said Seoras.

'No, we can't,' said Jane. Seoras felt his ankle being kicked. 'Time to go.'

'Okay,' said Seoras. The woman was almost fluttering her eyes at him. Her hand was still moving up and down his arm as Jane dragged him away. Seoras got the feeling he was being frog-marched up the street. As soon as they got past a residence, Jane pulled him to one side.

'What the hell's that?' she spat. 'You don't get to look at the candy. You don't get to stare. You don't get to—'

Seoras grabbed her and kissed her rather passionately. When

he broke off, it was as if Jane hadn't stopped talking. 'Wee tart like that, wee tart like that comes up in front of us and you don't just give her the brush off. You don't stand there and tell her how the love of your life is standing beside her, how the—'

Seoras put his finger up to her lips. 'Quiet,' he said. Then he hugged her and leaned in towards her ear. 'Would you explain to me why a woman of that age, looking like that, in their right mind, would come up to me? What woman would be interested in this body at that age?'

Jane paused for a moment. 'Well, I would.'

Seoras decided not to say, 'Well, you're not her age,' and instead continued his argument. 'The thing is that she clearly wanted something from us, maybe from me, wanted us to sit with her. I was going to find out what it was.'

Jane stared at him and squeezed his hand. 'Does this mean what I saw was real?'

'I don't know,' he said, 'but there's enough interest being taken in us that I will proceed as if it is real. Until I know better, we'll say it's real.'

'And you didn't want to go with her for any other reason?'

'What is this?' asked Seoras suddenly. 'You've got my undivided devotion, my attention. I've given up all my police work, told you it's you and me. I was just being protective, trying to find out what's going on.'

He was hurt, and it was only just dawning on her just how hurt he was.

'Sorry,' said Jane. 'But you're my man and nobody gets to do that. Nobody gets to—'

He smiled at her. 'I understand,' he said. 'But when we're investigating things, sometimes we have to do things we don't want to do or be people who we don't want to be. I just slip into it automatically. I forget sometimes you're not from my background. You haven't had the years of solving things. You haven't had—'

'No, but I could still have knocked her block off,' said Jane.

'And we wouldn't have got anywhere. We still haven't got anywhere. But that's okay. What you did is okay, because it makes it look like you're simply offended.'

'I was offended,' said Jane. 'I was offended, staring at her, saying you can go for a drink with her, saying it.'

'But I was acting.'

'Well, I realise that now, but she still had the audacity to come up and do it.'

'Because she wanted something out of me. And trust me, it wasn't for a night of passionate lovemaking. I think she might look elsewhere for that.'

'Does that mean I have to look elsewhere as well?' He laughed, reached forward and kissed her on the side of the cheek. 'Well, I can certainly carry over the threshold. Whether I get you any further along, I'm not sure if this body will make it.'

She punched him on the shoulder, smiled and stood while he tussled her hair. Seoras felt like a kid around her sometimes, and the two of them acted like kids. Was that the secret? Was that the way to go? Was that what they needed to do to be there for each other, to be that young spirit within?

They turned and held hands as they walked back down the dusty road before arriving at their hut. As they did so, they saw a vehicle outside with a red cross on it.

'What's he doing here?' asked Jane.

'Who is it?' asked Seoras.

'It's one of the doctors. One of the doctors from the medical centre.' She let go of Seoras' hand and walked up towards the vehicle, where the man got out, having seen them walk along the road.

'Forgive me for coming out,' he said.

'Is there a problem?' asked Jane.

'I just wanted to make sure you're all right.'

'Fine, I'm absolutely fine. We went out on the boat today, did some crabbing—well, Seoras did the crabbing. I kind of lay around the boat with him, just took it easy. When we brought it back, we went to the restaurant, had our dinner and now we're going to bed. It's getting pretty late for us. It's late also for you to be making a house call, isn't it?'

'I just wanted to make sure you're okay, that nothing else had happened. With being away most of the day and all that, we didn't have time to drop in on you.'

'If you had said,' interrupted Seoras, 'we would have made sure that Jane was available.'

'Do you mind if I give you an examination now?'

'Here in the street?' said Jane.

'No, no, no, just inside, if that's okay.'

'Okay,' said Jane. She watched how Seoras stepped back and let the doctor follow her in first. As he came up behind them, Seoras closed the front door and then sat in a seat a little distance away. Jane stood while the doctor carefully put down a bag.

'I'm just going to check the vitals,' he said. 'Blood pressure, all the rest.' He removed the monitor and the bandage strap to go around Jane's arm.

Seoras watched as the man performed what he thought to be a very basic examination. He checked her eyes; he checked her chest, up and down her back, legs, balance, and then declared that she seemed fully fit.

'So, have you remembered anything else,' he asked, 'about what went on when you were out there?'

'No,' said Jane. 'No, I just passed out.'

'Nothing at all. No images, nothing comes to mind. Nothing worrying you.'

'No,' said Jane. 'I had a very pleasant day, actually. I haven't done much.'

'Is that all?' asked Seoras. 'Really, she could do with bed more than anything else.'

'Well, I guess I'm just about finished up,' said the doctor. 'I just wanted to make sure that she was okay, and see if we could work out what had happened to her.'

'Well, she hasn't collapsed since,' said Seoras. 'Jane seems fighting fit at the moment. Eating well, drinking well. Everything looks good.'

'Yes,' said the doctor.

'Blood pressure okay?' asked Seoras.

'Yes,' said the doctor.

'Pupils okay? Chest okay? Everything looking okay?'

'I can't find anything wrong,' said the doctor. 'Maybe you could pop into the medical centre tomorrow?'

'With your leave, Jane,' said Seoras, 'I don't think that's necessary. It's not that we don't appreciate your coming out. It's not that we don't appreciate your checking up and making sure that all the I's are dotted and the T's are crossed, if you understand what that means. But I think we want to get on with our holiday now. If she has any recurrences or whatever, we'll come straight to you.'

'Well, I would like to—'

'Like I said,' said Seoras, 'we'll come straight to you.'

The doctor nodded, gave him a weak smile and gathered his belongings. He then left, and Seoras stood at the door watching as the car disappeared. Jane came up behind him, putting her hands on his shoulder.

'What do you make of that?' she asked.

'Don't trust him. There's nothing wrong with you. He told us nothing was wrong, and yet he lingers, still wanting to know what you saw. They don't know what's gone on, don't know if somebody saw something happening. They can't leave it either.'

'What do you mean?' asked Jane.

'If they'd seen you watching this man being murdered, you'd be dead. If they knew who you were, you'd be dead. Throw you off a cliff, something like that.'

'Charming,' said Jane.

'But they don't know that. They know someone's in the vicinity, or they know somebody's collapsed in the vicinity. When somebody sees someone being murdered, it's possible to go into shock, possible to collapse, if they're not used to it.'

'So, they need to find out what I know.'

'Exactly,' said Seoras. 'And they need to make sure that they don't have any reason to suspect that you know anything. So, you need to get to bed because that's what we said we were going to do. We are going to get you to bed and to relax.'

'And the woman,' said Jane, 'she was the same.'

'She would have been brought in to get us to talk, to get me to talk. I don't think they know who they're dealing with,' said Seoras. 'I don't think they recognise that I'm a DCI, or a former DCI.'

'So, what do we do?' said Jane.

'Well, for the moment, we get to bed. I need to think. We

63

need to find out what happened. If it truly happened, then what to do about it. Tomorrow, tomorrow we'll get on it, but for now, sleep. Let them see we're doing what they think we should be doing. Be the perfect holiday guests.'

She took his hand, pulling him away from the door, and led Seoras into the bedroom. Five minutes later, they were cuddled up in bed. He pulled her close, but he could feel it, the nervousness, the edginess within her. That wasn't Jane. Jane was deliberate, full of life. She saw it had to be done and did it. She didn't sweat what was coming. Jane didn't fret about it.

'You okay?' he asked.

'Yes,' she said, but Seoras knew it was a lie. He pulled her close.

'Trust me,' he said. 'I'll get to the bottom of it. I'll keep you safe.'

'Of course,' she said. 'My man's on the case. He'll solve it.'

Seoras hugged her tight again, but he was only half listening. His mind was elsewhere, working out how to solve this case.

Chapter 08

Jane awoke the next morning and found the bed to be empty. She put on her dressing gown and padded out into the living room beyond. She saw Seoras standing, looking out the window towards the sea. He didn't turn as she came up behind him and wrapped her arms around him, burying her chin into the back of his shoulders, right between the blades.

'You could have woken me.'

'No, I was thinking,' he said. 'Thinking about how best to do this.'

'I could have given you some input.'

'Go on then,' said Seoras.

'Well. I don't know; maybe we could.' She stopped, and she hit him. 'Don't ask me questions I can't answer.'

'No, love,' said Seoras. 'We're going to retrace your steps today.'

'That wise? You already went up to see where I had been. We know where I've been. You saw it from the boat.'

'We saw it from the boat,' said Seoras, 'but it's not the same. If we go, we might find out exactly where you've been. We might see things on the ground. We couldn't see up on the top of the cliffs. There are several reasons to do it. When you have nothing else, you backtrack, you replay the situation.'

'Is that one of your police things?' said Jane.

'Yes, it is actually.'

'But you're not in that role here,' said Jane. 'It's going to look odd if you prance about, isn't it?'

'I am aware of that. I also don't think we'll do it until later because the day is going to be very hot. If you and I must leg it, we want to be doing it in the cooler parts of the day, and we want to be doing it when night comes to hide us. So, we'll not head out this morning. We'll do a bit of shopping, sit and have coffee and whatever and come back late this afternoon and then go out.'

They made their way, after getting ready, to the small town centre. Seoras sat in the coffee shop while Jane went off to pick up some fruit. She wondered if it was wise, her being alone, but Seoras pointed out he could see the fruit stalls from the coffee shop. He also said that they needed to be apart at times, to show that they weren't afraid, that they didn't think that people were onto them, that there was anything untoward. Jane had nodded, but he knew she was nervous when she left him. As he sat sipping his coffee, the woman from the previous night suddenly slipped into the chair opposite him at the table.

'Hi,' she said. Her black hair was still hanging down loose, but now she was dressed in shorts and a rather tight t-shirt. She had Polaroid shades on, and there was that smile once more. 'Sorry to bother you,' she said. 'I just wanted to apologise. I obviously upset your wife.'

'Not at all,' said Seoras. 'And my partner. Jane's not my wife.'

'Oh,' said the woman. 'Is this some sort of illicit runaway?'

'No,' said Seoras. 'We're just not married.'

'Very modern,' said the woman.

'Just simpler. Got together later in life, it's just simpler. Anything I can help you with?' said Seoras.

The woman pulled her chair around, closer to him, and her legs were now sticking out to one side. He flashed a look down at them as if they'd grabbed his attention before looking back up to her. He saw the smile as if she'd trapped him like a spider looking at her web.

'Well, I just thought that maybe you'd like something else.'

'Like a latte?' said Seoras almost innocently.

'No, no. I mean, your partner's not here at the moment, is she?'

'She's in town,' said Seoras. He could see Jane at a distance buying fruit.

'That's a pity. Maybe you could find something for her to do. We don't get many men who look like you. Nice hat, by the way.'

Seoras put his hand up on top of the fedora and lifted it off, slowly, before putting it back down again. 'It's quite something, isn't it?'

'You've got quite a style about you,' said the woman.

Macleod had to control himself. Nobody had ever said that he had 'quite a style' about him. He'd been told he'd had no style, but never had it been mentioned in a positive way. He laughed inside and saw Jane coming back down the street.

'You'd better be scarce soon,' said Seoras. 'My partner's coming back. If she sees you here, she'll not be happy.'

'Well, if I see you about, maybe we could, you know.'

'Maybe,' said Seoras. And the woman walked off. Jane approached and sat down in the seat at the table and Seoras waved over a waiter, asking for a cappuccino for Jane.

'Was that the woman again?' asked Jane.

'Yes,' said Seoras. 'And believe it or not, she does want this body. Probably.'

'Well, she's not getting it,' said Jane.

'She actually complimented me on my style of dress, along with the fedora hat.'

'Well, somebody bought you that hat,' said Jane. 'And as for the rest of it, I didn't fall for your sense of style.'

'Seoras gave a smile. 'No,' said Seoras. 'Did you get the fruit?'

'I have enough for us. Let's head back. We'll have a rest before we go out,' said Jane.

Seoras nodded, and after Jane had drunk her coffee, they walked back to their hut. After having a doze for a couple of hours, the pair headed out. Seoras carried a rucksack on his back with enough supplies for their trip.

Although the day was more than half done, the heat was still strong and they took it carefully as they retraced Jane's steps across the island. Eventually, it was dark by the time they got to the compound. They could see it in the distance. Seoras thought about walking down the rock path to the place where Jane had been before, from which she had seen the man being killed. He looked around him and then he told Jane to take out a blanket.

'A blanket,' she said. 'What for?'

'Just put it down.' He sat down on it and pulled Jane down. Taking out some of the food, they sat eating, and Seoras told Jane to look up at the stars.

'You want me to look at the stars,' she said. 'Why?'

'Because it's romantic,' said Seoras. 'I've just been propositioned by a younger woman today. I didn't blow her off. I told her I might be interested. So, I'm out here with you on a guilt trip, doing something romantic, looking at the stars. So, look at the stars with me.'

Jane looked up and felt Seoras pull her close. He lay back slightly, allowing her to lean on him. Then he pointed up at the sky. He laughed a little, and she had no idea why. So, she laughed with him.

'We're not even staring at the compound. We haven't got the—'

'Shush,' said Seoras. 'Just trust me and look at the stars.'

Together they sat, eating, and then cuddling. Seoras looked around him though, carefully, out of the corner of his eye. He wasn't happy. When he had the idea of retracing Jane's steps, he thought it wouldn't be that difficult. And indeed, it wasn't. Nobody had stopped him. In fact, it was too easy. Maybe that was it. Maybe someone else was looking to see where she had gone.

There was a rustle nearby, and Seoras grabbed Jane, kissing her deeply. When she went to break off, he wouldn't let her. She took the hint and kissed him back.

There were footsteps now, close, but Seoras kept Jane in tight until suddenly he heard a cough.

The pair broke apart suddenly, as if disturbed by a peeping Tom. Seoras turned around with an angry face. There was a guard standing with a gun. In the distance, he thought he saw another one.

'Do you mind?' said Seoras. 'We're just here trying to enjoy the stars; here trying to enjoy each other, to get a bit of time away from everyone.'

'What are you doing?' asked the guard. 'What do you mean by time away?'

Seoras stood up and led the man a few feet away. 'Woman?

Me,' he said. 'Go into the town and the bars and it's all noise. People about everywhere. Here? On our own. I have the stars. I have food. I have everything to make her happy. Except you. You barge in. Do you know what it's like?' said Seoras. 'Do you know how a woman is turned off if you point a gun at her? If she sees men in combat gear?'

'Why up here, though?' asked the man.

'There's nobody else about until you came. That's why. I just want to sit and look at the stars with her. Get her in the mood.'

The man leaned across, looked at Jane, and then at Seoras. 'Aren't you a bit old to get in the mood?'

'What? What age are you?' asked Seoras.

'Thirty-five,' said the man.

'I am as much in the mood nowadays as I was back then.' He leant in close. 'Yes, she can take a lot more warming up.' And then he leaned back away from the man, put a hand up to his head and tapped it. 'When you're older,' he whispered. 'You've got to work the mood a lot more. You know? Worth it. But you know.' The man nodded. 'So?' said Seoras. 'Are you going?'

'How much longer are you going to be here?'

'An hour? But I don't want somebody watching us.'

'We patrol around here,' said the man. 'Around the compound. Just need to know what people are doing.'

'Well, I've explained myself,' said Seoras. 'Do you need money?'

The guard waved his hand. 'No, no, no. I'll go now,' he said. 'Good luck.'

Seoras nearly burst out laughing as he turned away from the guard. But he didn't, and instead sat down beside Jane, pulling her close again. He kissed her and then whispered in her ear.

'There are guards everywhere,' he said. 'Those will be the ones sent out. We're being watched. We're not going to do much else here. What we're going to do is sit and look at the stars for an hour.'

'That sounds good,' said Jane. She took his hand.

'I actually told him I was looking to . . . well, you know.'

'Get your leg over,' said Jane bluntly.

'I wouldn't have put it so delicately,' said Seoras.

Jane sniggered. 'You really struggle with things like that, don't you?' she said.

'I'm not playing a part when I'm talking to you. I could have said that to the man there. It wouldn't have bothered me.' He pulled her close again, his head on her shoulder, and his eyes were scanning out all around.

He remembered Kirsten, the detective he'd worked with in his early days of coming to Inverness. She'd gone off to the Secret Service and saved his life several times. Kirsten could scan around, see people. He hadn't spotted them when they arrived. He'd laid a trap and pulled them out. Seoras had been patient, but unlike Kirsten, he couldn't hide. Not in plain sight.

How he wished he had Kirsten with him now. Kirsten could get this done in an instant. And more than that, if they got into trouble, she could get them out of it. But it was up to him and Jane, nobody else.

They sat there cuddling for about an hour and then he stood up, taking Jane, packing up the blanket and putting the rucksack on his back. As they left, he turned around and shouted, 'Cheers, guys,' in a rather ironic voice. He saw the movement. A guard who came out from behind a bush and gave him an acknowledgement. Clearly, they'd missed the sarcasm.

As they walked back through the cooler night, Seoras stayed close to Jane. It would not be that easy. It wasn't just a case of following in her footsteps. When he'd been a detective inspector, he'd gone where he'd wanted to a large degree. You were the police; you could just get in there. You could stop other people, clear a path. Jona, the forensic lead, would have been out with her tape. Police crime scene. Do not cross. All the rest of it.

But not her. Here he was on his own with his wits, and his wit had saved them. For his wit had drawn out the fact they'd been watched. They might have to do it differently. They might have to leave it for a day or two. Truly blend back in. They had only about a week and a half left. And in a week and a half, would he be able to convince them he'd seen nothing? Would he be able to find out what had happened?

He was worried for their safety, but as ever, his first thought was on stopping murderers. His first thought was to bring justice. It was going to be harder. He didn't have a team to help him. He didn't have a team to cover his weaknesses. What he had was a very keen and very loyal partner. But he didn't know if that would be enough.

Chapter 09

Seoras had decided that they needed to step back a little, believing this may be a longer investigation. They couldn't simply retrace steps because they were being watched. So, he decided that to take the heat off, they would need to step back for a day or two. He also told Jane that she needed to head off into town on her own. The one thing they needed to do was not look worried, not look harassed, as if they knew something. Instead, they needed to act as if they were making the most of their holiday. The next day, Seoras headed down to the beach and lay down on a towel. Jane headed off into town to pick up some more food.

The fruit on the island was truly amazing, and it was for that she headed to the fruit stalls. The day was packed with sunshine, so much you could feel the sweat dripping off her forehead. She wore a t-shirt with a light blouse and some shorts below. Jane was doing her best just to enjoy herself. She stopped at several smaller shops on the way where there were occasional knick-knacks to pick up, and she bought a few, thinking of people back home. She was, however, worried.

Seoras was out on his own, but he knew how to handle himself. She'd always thought he was clever, but now she was seeing him in action, truly in action. The way he had got her to sit down, look at the stars—it was like he had a sixth sense. He knew something was up. Maybe he just saw the signs better.

He was missing Hope, the detective inspector he'd worked with for all those years. Jane had always wondered about Seoras and Hope. They always seemed so close, but they were many years apart, well over twenty. And yet it never seemed like a father-daughter type of friendship. Hope was fast. Strong as well. Six feet tall. An action-type woman. Seoras was more of a thinking man.

Jane wasn't sure if in his earlier days he'd been that much of an action man either. She realised she couldn't be Hope, and nor would she want to be, as much as she liked the woman. Jane was herself—bubbly, punchy. She brought out a side in Seoras that Hope never could. But how that helped them now in the investigation she didn't know. For she was now his partner, in the investigation as well as in life. What could she do to help him?

As she picked up some fruit, Jane realised she was being watched by a middle-aged man. He had a rather prominent belly that was being held in by a T-shirt. And when she looked up, he gave her an enormous smile and started wandering over towards her.

'You know what my own mother would say? My own mother would say that you're a heck of a woman. The way you pick out that fruit—do you see what you're doing there? You don't buy just anything. You test everything. There's a good man behind you. A good man is getting fed well and being looked after.'

'Excuse me?' said Jane.

'Oh, forgive me. Big mouth, talking awfully like that. Sorry, did I give you a shock? I don't mean to. I really don't mean to. Just saying that me mam at home would have loved the way you've done that. You know? Sorry, I'm a bit familiar, aren't I?'

'Well, you're certainly more forward than many people here,' said Jane. She'd thought about what Seoras had said about the woman, and how she was appealing to the sexual side of his nature. This man was firing compliments at Jane like they were going out of fashion. She became wary.

'You here for a while?' he asked.

'Well, we've been here for the best part of three or four days,' said Jane.

'Yes. Yes, I've seen you. How was the crabbing?'

'The crabbing?' asked Jane.

'Yes, I saw you from my boat. You went out crabbing. You and the man you're with. Is that your fella? Or is that someone else? Your brother, maybe?'

'No, no,' said Jane. 'That's my man.'

'You're picking all this fruit out for him? That's quite something,' said the man. He sounded Irish. 'I'm so sorry; I should have introduced myself. My name's Eamon. Eamon, and you can probably tell I'm from Ireland, although I haven't been back around Ireland in a while now. You're English, aren't you? I can hear that in that voice.'

'I am, but my partner's Scottish.'

'An English rose,' said Eamon. 'You walk around here, and you know, wherever you go, half of them are parading around with nothing on. Sure it's wild. Youngsters, you know, twenty, thirty-year-old youngsters. All looking the part and guys chasing after them. But you have to look hard to find a real woman, a woman like yourself, not just brains and beauty. A bit more.'

75

'You can tell that from me just buying fruit?' said Jane.

'And that's what I like about you,' said Eamon, laughing. 'Little quips like that, you know. Your man's good to you though, isn't he? Did you enjoy your stargazing?'

Jane felt a cold streak run down the back of her neck. How did he know about the stargazing? Going out in the boat, crabbing, coming back in and giving them to the restaurant. She understood that she could have been seen then. That made sense, but the stargazing? There were only the guards out there. Her, Seoras and the guards. How did he know about that?

'You keeping an eye on me?' asked Jane.

'What man wouldn't keep an eye on you? If that bloke of yours ever gets fed up with you, which I don't know how, I'm right here, love. You're a fine, grand woman.'

'Well, that's forward,' she said. 'But you know, live and let live.' She took the fruit now and walked over to the counter and found Eamon was following behind her. She placed it down to pay for it before popping it in a string bag. Eamon quickly paid for his goods behind her. but Jane was away and out onto the street. So quickly, that she almost collided with the medical vehicle sitting there.

'Forgive me,' said a voice.

It was the doctor, the one who had been sitting outside her hut two nights ago.

'Hello,' said Jane. 'I'm fine.'

'I thought we should have a check-up, though. Would you like to come with me to the health centre now? We'll go back in and we'll just have a quick look, see what's wrong.'

'There's nothing wrong,' said Jane. 'I'm feeling fine.'

'Do you remember anything else?'

'No. No, I just collapsed, I told you. I don't remember anything.'

'Well, I must insist,' said the doctor. 'I must insist that you come with me. We need to maybe do some hypnotherapy. Take a look back.'

'What's your game, sunshine?' cried a voice. It was Eamon, holding a large watermelon under his arm.

'Do you mind?' said the doctor. 'This is a medical examination.'

'In the street?' said Eamon. 'I think you're short on the rent this month. You don't examine a woman on the street. Do you know this man?'

Jane recognised the absurdity of the question, because she barely knew Eamon at all.

'I had a little collapse at the start of the holiday, and this is one of the doctors who helped look after me. But I'm fine now. I've told them I'm fine.'

'She is radiating health. Look at her. Doc, look at her. What a fantastic woman! She is absolutely brimming. That brown hair, look at it.'

'This is none of your business,' said the doctor curtly. 'None at all.'

'Well, be off with you then,' said Eamon. 'Be off with you.'

'If you'll listen to me,' the doctor said to Jane, 'Miss Hislop, I can take you.'

'I haven't got Seoras with me,' said Jane. 'I need to see Seoras.'

'I can take you in. We'll get word to him. He can come along afterwards,' said the doctor.

Jane felt another cold streak running down the back of her neck. She didn't know who Eamon was, but he clearly didn't want what the doctor wanted. And the doctor seemed to want the same thing he'd wanted all along, to know if she remembered anything.

'I've told you, doctor, I don't know anything. I can't remember any of that.'

'Well, we can try hypnotherapy. We can find out what happened. We can find out if you've had a fall, if you've—'

'She is in fine fettle,' said Eamon, coming up and putting his arm around Jane's shoulders. 'Look at her. You don't need to go anywhere. In fact, you should come with me for a drink. Would you like to go to the cafe? Let's go to the cafe and have a drink.'

'I should probably get back to Seoras.'

'Well, we can get Seoras as well,' said Eamon. 'Do you know something, Jane? I always think that these medical people, they just want to get hold of you so they can prod you. They can use their instruments. Get some tablets into you. There'll probably be a stinking great bill at the end of it when everybody can see that you're in terrific form. Look at you, ready to munch down on the fruit there. You've got everything going. You just need a wee cuppa. Come with me.'

Eamon put his arm through Jane's arm. 'And Doc, would you just leave the woman alone? She knows where the medical centre is. If she needs help, she'll come. At the moment, she's grand and she's not felt the need to come and say anything to you. I'm sure her man's looking after her, and I'm going to look after her now and get her a coffee. So we don't have to worry about her. And then I'll get her back to her man, Okay, skipper?'

'This is none of your business,' said the doctor.

'I tend to agree with Eamon here,' said Jane. She turned and smiled at him. 'Best thing for me is to have a bit of enjoyment, a nice coffee, and relax. I don't need to be pushed, prodded, and I certainly don't need any hypnotherapy. If I need you, Doc, I'll call. Good day.'

Jane felt Eamon walk before she did, and he almost whisked her across the road. It was only a few hundred yards down to the coffee house, and Eamon said nothing until they got onto the veranda. But Jane noticed he watched to make sure the doctor disappeared. Then he turned and smiled at her.

'What would you like?'

'No,' said Jane. 'I'm going to get you a coffee for that rescue.'

'They're unbelievable, aren't they?' said Eamon. 'Just unbelievable. You tell them one thing, but they think they know best. I mean, you know when you feel good, don't you? I do. I felt good the moment I saw you. But that's men, isn't it? We see a good-looking woman, a nice, fresh, bubbly woman, and suddenly our pep's up. We feel good, you know? You, for whatever reason today—maybe it was the sunshine—you feel good. So, let me get you a coffee.'

'No,' said Jane. 'I will not let you buy me one. I'm going to buy you one, and Seoras will hear how you rescued me.'

'So, your Seoras, he's quite a man, is he? That'll be a pity,' said Eamon. 'But, by all means, I'll have a mocha.'

Jane nodded and waved over one of the waiters, ordering a cappuccino for herself, along with a mocha for Eamon. She sat back in the seat and stared at the man. He had an enormous grin on his face, and his chair was turned sideways so he could almost lie sideways to look at her.

'Are you always this bubbly with people?'

'I think you're rather bubbly yourself,' said Eamon. 'I'll be honest with you. I have a boat here, and I do some work around the island, doing different things, and I love the sun.

But I don't always get to meet people from home.'

'I'm from England.'

'We're on the other side of the world,' said Eamon. 'England, Ireland, Scotland, Wales, Channel Islands. Anywhere around there, that's home. You speak English like I speak English.'

Jane laughed a little. 'The trouble out here,' he said, 'is they're different. Especially on this island. I don't know; they seem to like things to run smoothly. They certainly don't get sarcasm, you know? They don't. And their English is, well, it's good, but it's not like we speak it. They can't yabber together, you know? Bit of banter, bit of back and forward. Ah,' he said, 'the coffees.'

Jane watched as the man slid two sugars into his coffee, stirring it, and then lifted it towards her. 'Thank you,' he said. 'Cheers.' Jane sipped on her cappuccino, watching him carefully.

'So, you've got a boat,' she said. 'You watched us from your boat.'

'Yes, I have a boat. You must come for dinner.'

'I'm afraid I'll have to bring Seoras if you want me to come for dinner. I'm not going off with another man for dinner. That won't go down well.'

'Oh, bring him. Bring him,' said Eamon. 'Don't get me wrong. Look, you took me back there in the fruit shop. I saw this woman with the striking brunette hair and I thought, wow, look at her. You just ooze life, you know? And I struggle here. You see, a lot of the women in there, well, they're full of themselves. They want to know how they look and that. You don't. You're a bundle of fire. See her there,' he said pointing to a woman behind the coffee house bar, 'she is lively too. Slightly different, comes from a different age, but I can sit and have a coffee with her and have a bit of talk and banter and everybody's great. I think you're the same.'

'What type of boat do you have?' asked Jane.

'The boat? Oh, you'll love the boat. I live on my boat here. Don't have a villa. I'm one of the ones who have a spot in the harbour. I just came down here to get away. It's the sunshine. I don't like the cold at home anymore, but I miss the people. You know everybody talks about Ireland, and Ireland is the countryside and the rolling fields of green. It isn't. Ireland is the people. And when we're not blowing the hell out of each other, we're actually really good fun. You're good fun too. I always liked the English. The English are different though, you know. Good friends though. Good friends. I've got some good English friends. The Americans, not so much. No, but they're not from home. You know how it is.

'We've mixed so much nowadays, haven't we? Well it used to be that you went nowhere, but look at me now. Other side of the world.' Jane sat and listened to him babble on about home and what he would make for dinner before she'd finished her cup and then stood up.

'Come for dinner. Yes. Couple of days. Bring your man with you,' said Eamon. 'It'll be a delight.' As she went to walk off, he stepped over and gave her a hug. 'Take care,' he said. 'We'll see you soon.'

As Jane left, she had the funniest feeling. The man talked as if he'd known her all his life, but clearly he hadn't. And yet, he'd said earlier on about the stargazing. She wasn't sure what to make of him. There was warmth, but there was also mystery. He never asked her for anything. Never asked her about what she'd seen or anything like that. So maybe he differed from the others. Maybe not. She wondered what Seoras would make of it.

Chapter 10

Seoras put the fedora on his head and looked out into the sunshine. Behind him, he could hear Jane picking up his rucksack and bringing it over to him.

'Are you sure you want to do this?'

'If I go out there with you and retrace your path with you, they'll think that's what I'm doing. If I go out walking myself and come back to your path, leave it and come back, leave it and come back, I could get away with retracing your steps without them noticing. At least, that's what I reckon.'

'But they had all those guards out, didn't they, last time?'

'Well, we've waited a day or two, now. Yesterday, nobody came from the medical centre to say anything to you. Nobody said anything to me. Maybe they've left us. Best if I try to push that theory on my own.'

'Why?' asked Jane. He turned around and saw a rather worried face.

'Because if there's trouble, I'll handle it.'

'How? You don't have a team around you. Don't have all your detective constables, detective sergeants. You don't have Kirsten ready to jump in for you. It's just you.'

'And it was me long before I had all of them around me,

working the streets of Glasgow on my own.'

'You were younger then. A good bit younger.' He gave a smile, but he could see she was worried. 'Seoras, are we going to get out of here? Are we going to get clear? In another week or so, we're going anyway. Will they stop us? Will they make a move by then if they think I've seen something?'

'They don't know if you've seen something. If they had believed you had seen it, we wouldn't be here. They're weighing that risk. No point in rocking the boat if nothing's been seen.'

'But the constant questions.'

'They're trying to break us down. They're trying to see if we flinch. React like someone who's just annoyed at their overexuberance, not someone who's trying to hide something.'

'I don't like this side of things.'

'That's because you're not an actor like me.'

'An actor like you? When have you ever acted?' said Jane. 'You don't do the stage. You hate panto. The theatre. Well, you only get to the theatre when I drag you. And last time, somebody got shot dead at it.'

'I act all the time,' said Seoras quietly. 'Every interview I go into is an act. And when I speak to people, it's an act. I'm a detective. Chief inspector. It's not wholly me. Like any good actor, there's a part of me in it. And this is a different role now, and you put yourself into it. You're doing great, love. Keep it together.'

'You want me just to sit on the beach?'

'Yes,' said Seoras. 'It's very public, so they can't do anything. But you're also showing that you're not hiding away. Take yourself down to the coffee shop. Take yourself to the restaurant. When they ask, tell them I'm hiking. I enjoy it.

Make it normal. Always make it normal.'

He pushed the hat down onto his head, took the rucksack off her and slung it over both shoulders. 'I'll be fine,' he said.

He bent down, and she kissed him. And then she hugged him tight. 'Take care,' she said.

A few minutes later, Seoras was walking off into the scrubland in the middle of the island. He deliberately started off on a different path from the one Jane had taken that fateful morning. Instead, he went off at an angle, wandering along paths as if he didn't care where he was going. But he checked, and in his head, he knew where the paths went. He cut back, heading back to the path that she had taken, gradually picking up her steps here and there before breaking off again and then coming back to them.

He looked like he was wandering. Every now and again he would stop to look at something. Often they were innocuous things, but he would look over his shoulder to see if anyone was following. He saw them now and again. There was a helicopter that passed above him. Of course, he couldn't be sure. Maybe he was under a sensible flight path. They were certainly keeping an eye on him, or so he believed.

As he got close, back towards Jane's path from that fateful morning, he saw some gravestones and casually wandered over. These were the graves Jane had mentioned. As he stood reading what was on them, he struggled to make sense of anything beyond names or possibly years. Seoras looked around him again. No one. Then something caught his eye. One of the graves. Well, it didn't look right.

In his time as a police officer, he'd seen some rapidly dug graves, some done very well to hide bodies, some done poorly. This was a decent effort, but it was far from perfect. The headstone said that the grave was at least sixty years old, or at least the body in it was. He thought maybe he should bend down and have a look, but he got a feeling he was being watched. Seoras couldn't say from where; he couldn't say who was doing it, but something inside him tingled.

He turned and walked on, going nearly a good half a mile away and then stopped as if he'd gone down the wrong track, turned back and retraced his steps to the grave. Just before he arrived, he saw someone on the ground.

She was lying sunbathing, and as he got closer, he realised that she really had next to nothing on. It was the woman who had sought his protection in the town.

'Hello,' she said, sitting up on her elbows now and confirming what Seoras had thought. She had on a small thong, and that was it, and she was smiling at him.

'My apologies. I didn't mean to disturb you,' said Seoras. He went to walk past, and the woman sat up further. Rather than covering herself up, she was almost positioning herself so he could have a good look. He averted his eyes. 'I'll just be on my way,' he said.

'Something wrong?' asked the woman. 'You're not a prude, are you?'

'How you want to dress is up to yourself. There's only one woman in my life, though.'

'Would you like a drink? It can't hurt you to sit down and have a drink with me.'

'I don't drink,' said Seoras. And it was the truth. He hadn't touched alcohol for years. Brought up hearing it as the demon drink, he'd taken that to heart and never really got on to drinking. Once or twice in his young days, but never since.

'Something's wrong,' she said. 'You prefer redheads, do you?'

Seoras turned and looked at her, focusing on the eyes staring back at him. She was almost daring him to sit down with her, daring him to take time now.

He could see the attraction. He was a man, after all, and she was certainly a woman. Seoras fixed his eyes on her face, looking to read what was there. It was insane. Why would a woman like this be throwing herself at him? Unless she desperately thought he had a lot of money, which he didn't. Or she needed to find out something from him. Why were they trying to split Jane and him apart? Maybe get him to talk? To say what she'd seen? It wasn't subtle. It was incredibly coarse.

'I like redheads,' he said. 'Brunettes too. Actually, any colour except pink. And a woman with a little, well, pride in herself. I don't like women who throw themselves at me.'

The woman stared back, daring him to follow through on what he had just said, and Seoras did, turning away and walking on past her. The graves were just on the other side of her, though. That's what he wanted. He wanted to go there and look at that grave. And then suddenly she pitched up here, with next to nothing on, trying to entice him. In fact, not trying to entice him—offering herself on a plate.

As he walked away from the graves, he felt for sure something was there. Once he went down a small hollow away from the graves, he sat down, keeping himself out of sight. The hollow allowed him to almost stand without being seen, and he peered up over the edge occasionally.

The woman didn't stay long after he'd gone past before getting up, throwing on a shirt, and then walking off with her towel and bag. When she got maybe two hundred yards down the path, a small Jeep rolled up, picked her up, and drove her away.

Quickly, Seoras scrambled back over to the graves. He bent down at the one he had noticed before. Looking around him, he brushed the soil away, parched as it was, revealing more upturned soil beneath. Graves were compact. If they'd been there for a while, they'd have compacted. This was freshly dug. He was sure of it.

Seoras wondered what he should do. Should he dig? That was the way to find a body. Get the shovels out. Dig down. He remembered having to exhume bodies, and the palava of the diggers and the people with the spades. All the forms to do it. Now here he was, ready to simply get a spade and dig. Of course, he didn't do the digging back then. Somebody else did the digging for him. Seoras tried to remember what it was like to dig that deep.

He pushed his hands into the soil, getting them in as far as he could. But he couldn't find anything. Even a shallow grave had a good couple of inches of soil above it. Seoras' heart was thumping, and he could hear a helicopter in the distance. He picked himself up and walked away from the graves, down towards the hollow. As he got there, he thought about a bush beside him. With a quick scan, he still couldn't see the helicopter, so he clambered down under the bush and froze there. The helicopter swung by. Once it was out of sight, Seoras turned and hurried back to the grave again.

What should he do now? He didn't think they'd actually put the man in a grave. A grave? Not here. Why not chuck him out into the sea? Of course he could wash up then. Would he wash up in the right places?

But here? With gravestones that were sixty, seventy, eighty, or a hundred years old. Nobody would go looking for him. Not here. That's if anybody missed him at all.

Macleod readjusted his backpack and headed back to Jane. The sun was blazing. He thought about the woman who had tried to stop him and then he wondered if this was a ploy. She was coarse. Not a subtle treat waiting to pull you away to one side. No, no, they turned up and put the jam doughnut right in front of his face. Because that's what it was like. All sugar. No sweetener. Unadulterated, pure sugar. There to be had.

They probably thought he would jump at the chance. He would need to come back. He would need to come back with a spade. But he couldn't just buy a spade. He'd have to get one. If he knew there was a body there, it would prove what Jane had seen. Although at the moment he felt he knew that Jane had seen something. After all, these people, they were working so hard to see what she knew. Working so hard to find out where she'd been. He sipped water from his backpack as he continued to walk back, eventually reaching the town again.

He dropped the bag into the house and then wandered out to the beach, where Jane was lying sunbathing. However, she was certainly much more covered up than the last sunbather he'd seen. He sat down beside her.

'You okay?' she said. 'Enjoy your walk?'

'I was . . . well.' He started and then he stopped.

'What?' she said.

'Remember that woman? The one you wanted to hit? The one who was kind of offering herself to me.'

'It's kind of hard to forget her,' said Jane. 'What about her?'

'I was walking, and I spotted something. I walked past and then turned because I thought I was being watched. Then, when I came back, she was sunbathing.'

'Sunbathing?' said Jane.

'Yes. European style.'

'What do you mean, European style? There's a European style of sunbathing?'

'Bottoms only,' said Seoras.

'What? She—'

'She offered me a drink, wanted me to sit down with her. And then she asked if I preferred redheads.'

'If I get hold of her; if I—'

'No,' said Seoras suddenly. 'You don't talk about it, but redheads. Some people have been doing a bit of research.'

'You said you spotted something though. I take it you just said no to her. I take it you haven't made love to her to find out what she knows.'

'No,' said Seoras. 'Her loss, obviously.'

Jane hit him on the arm.

'Are you saying it isn't? Are you saying she wouldn't have been impressed?'

'When I said I wanted a new you, when I said leave the detective behind,' said Jane, 'I didn't mean—'

'What? I can be funny when I want to,' said Seoras.

'What did you find?'

'Well, I left her. I went and hid and then came back. At the graveyard you passed, one of the graves didn't look right. Not the right amount of soil. It was disturbed. Said it was a sixty-year-old grave as well. Absolute nonsense. It's freshly dug.'

'Was there a body in it?'

'I only had my hands. I need to get a spade onto it. Probably not be able to do it in daylight either. It's a bit obvious.'

'So, what do we do?'

'Let me think,' he said. 'Let me think.'

'Well, you can think as much as you want, but we're off to Eamon's tonight. At least I won't have to cook.'

'I wonder who he is,' said Seoras.

'He might just be a nice guy.'

'But he's been watching us,' said Seoras.

'You're not the only one who can attract people. Maybe he likes this young filly here beside you.'

'Well, he hasn't got a chance,' said Seoras.

'That's very manly of you.'

'No, I mean, you're not going to resist this body beside you, are you?' he said. She hit him, and he laughed, reaching over and cuddling her.

As they tightened together, Jane said to him, 'I'm scared. I have lain here today watching everything, watching for people coming for me, watching for people.'

'Shush,' said Seoras. 'You can't do that. Focus on the problem. Focus on how to solve it, not on the fear. The fear will paralyse you. We'll get there, trust me. I may have said goodbye to the detective chief inspector but he never truly went. He's always here. Always.'

Chapter 11

'Ah, good on yous. Good to see you. Come in, come in, come in. Onto the boat, onto the boat, come on.'

Jane walked ahead of Seoras and took Eamon's hand as he helped her on board his yacht. Seoras followed, and the man shook his hand as if it had been something he'd wanted to do for his entire life.

'Now that is some hat,' said Eamon. 'Look at it. Wish I could wear a hat like that. But you have to have one of those faces, don't you? That serious, brooding face.'

'Some people wouldn't take that as a compliment,' said Jane.

'Oh, I mean it entirely as a compliment. There's character; there's depth in that face, isn't there? Eamon, by the way.'

'Seoras, Seoras Macleod.'

'Well, thank you for coming. I'm glad you've come as well. I didn't want you to think that I was trying to steal your woman, although I've got to be honest, if you weren't here, I'd jump at the chance.'

Seoras saw Jane smile at that. He thought it must be nice at her age to have someone compliment her so openly, and yet Eamon was almost cheeky. The man had a way about him. He had the ability to almost laugh at everything, to make everything a compliment, not a sneer or a crude remark. Seoras thought if he came off with that remark, it would either fall flat or be taken completely the wrong way.

'I'm going to take the yacht out a little, then anchor up. We'll have our dinner out there. I hope you like seafood. Obviously, this is a place for seafood. You were crabbing the other day yourselves, weren't you?'

'We were,' said Seoras. 'To be honest, I'm not much of a fisherman. I haven't done it for a long while, but the crabbing was good.'

'You're a lucky man, too,' said Eamon. 'Doesn't she look terrific tonight?'

'That I am,' said Seoras. He put an arm around Jane's waist, pulling her in tight.

Eamon smiled. 'Oh, don't worry. Don't worry, I'll charm her, but I'm not after her. Well, not yet.'

He took them up to the bridge of his yacht and steered the vessel a short distance out from shore before dropping anchor. He then served them wine and was shocked when Seoras said he wouldn't have any. There was fruit juice, however, and soon the three of them were standing in the galley while Eamon cooked.

'It's fish, and a lot of local vegetables and that, but I think I do all right,' he said.

Seoras looked at the spice rack and the various other ingredients kicking about and was incredibly impressed. He wasn't one for making fancy meals. He certainly didn't understand some of the names. But he could smell, and what was coming from the pan smelt delicious, producing an incredible aroma. It wasn't long before they were sitting on the deck at the back of the boat, eating. A pudding arrived later and Eamon cleared away before conducting them to another level of the yacht. There was a large sofa, Jane sat on and Eamon sat opposite, leaving Seoras to squeeze in beside her.

'Well, what in the blazes are you doing out here? Seoras Macleod. Now that's a Scottish name.'

'Well, we're off enjoying life. I'm recently retired,' said Seoras.

'Retired? What did you do?'

'I'm a former policeman,' said Seoras. He knew that with the redhead comment the woman had made that people might actually know what he was. Better to play a straight bat and not give too much information. Always best if they heard you say something they could collaborate.

'Well, you're certainly away from it all over here,' said Eamon.

'You been out here long yourself?' asked Seoras.

'Three years. Three years with my boat, my savings here. I had a, well, rather unfortunate marriage. I say that because we drove each other insane, and then I saw someone else; she saw someone else, then we kept trying to get it back together, and in the end, we gave up.'

'It's quite a yacht though.'

'It is, but I don't have that much money. I sailed it all the way over here from Ireland. Been here three years. Took months to get here though.'

'So, what do you do?' asked Seoras.

'I have a pension back in Ireland. It pays in and I can live off it. It doesn't cost much to live here. The boat needs the odd bit of work, but when we sold the house we had, because I was in finance, I got me a good pot. A good pot that I now live off. I don't want to be bothered with work anymore. And I enjoy it here. The views are good. There's plenty of younger people too. I like to be around young people. Don't get me wrong. I love talking to you two. But younger people make you feel young yourself, don't they? They make you feel you're not—'

'Past it,' said Jane. 'But it's hard to keep up with the pace of them. We saw a couple on our first night. Do you remember, Seoras? We were out on the beach, and these two just ran starkers into the sea.'

'Oh, that's what it's like here. People feel free to do what they want. I mean, within the limits, of course. I mean, nothing too daft. But they're not that worked up on the island with things like that. And if you do something a bit too much, well, they have a word. They have a word indeed. They come round, take you to one side, and, well, if you don't behave, then you're away. Seen a few people moved on.'

'Moved on,' said Seoras.

'Ah, there's the policeman in him, looking to see how they moved on. Taken out in a boat, dropped into the ocean. That's what you'd be expecting, isn't it?'

'That's what they used to say about where I was from,' said Seoras. 'Back in the day, people who were terrible, who really had done things, were dressed up in their best Sunday suit. Out in the boat, middle of the Minch, and dropped. Recorded as having disappeared. Or so the tales went.'

'Well, my island's had a bit of a history as well, making people disappear every now and again,' said Eamon. 'Well, they're not like that here. Stick them on a plane back to the Seychelles, and then they can make their way on, or their boats are not welcome. Been three years here now. Three years of watching the wildlife.' He laughed at that one. 'They are wild, some of them.'

'Well, it's funny,' said Jane, 'because it has that island feel, and

95

yet they have that thing at the other end.'

'Oh, the compound,' said Eamon. 'The compound brings the money in. That's why they can afford the island.'

'What's produced there?' asked Seoras.

'High end chemicals,' said Eamon. 'Yes, there's a few corners cut and that. Don't have to measure up to certain regs so they can produce them slightly cheaper, but people don't care. They get their chemicals at a good price. He gets the money. It's his island.'

'But that must be quite something. I mean, chemicals can be got anywhere. It can't be that cheap to bring them here,' said Seoras.

'Oh, you want the actual story. You see, that is a policeman. You see that, Jane? That's the policeman you're with. I hope you hide nothing from him because he'll find it out. He'll ask and ask and prod and prod until you tell him.'

'Oh, don't worry. I can handle him.'

Eamon stood up laughing, and grabbed his drink. 'I bet she can.' He grabbed a bottle of wine, walked over and poured Jane some more. Her cheeks were becoming flushed, Seoras noted, but she was more relaxed here. He wasn't sure if Eamon was a problem or not. He felt Eamon was holding something back, and his jovial manner made it difficult to prod.

'What about money, though?' said Seoras. 'It must be difficult? You can't make money being all the way out here.'

'Well, it's the chemicals that other countries tend not to produce—unethical ones, dangerous ones. Make them here and then sell them on.'

'And that's how they got the island. I mean, it was bought, was it?'

'Owns the entire island, the man who built the compound.

You don't see him very often, keeps himself to himself. Has a big high-end-falutin building up there somewhere for himself but doesn't interfere with the island. And the island life is what I like; get down off your boat, enjoy the sunshine, sit and have coffee, see some people here. The ones that have stayed over the three years, they produce what's good. You don't want to come here and get second best; you don't want to come here and get rubbish, do you?' said Eamon.

'The coffee's certainly excellent,' said Seoras.

'Ah, is he a man who knows his coffee?' asked Eamon.

'Don't start him,' said Jane. 'You get him on coffee, he won't shut up; trust me, he won't shut up. Will you, dear?'

She turned and kissed him on the cheek, and Seoras could tell she'd had a few too many. She wasn't out of control, but she was certainly happier, freer.

'I'll tell you one thing, though,' said Seoras. 'Since I've been here, Jane nearly clobbered someone.'

'Oh,' said Eamon, 'clobbered someone. I can tell why. I mean, don't mind my saying, but you look a feisty wee one.'

Jane sniggered. 'You're just lucky I'm not closer to you. You'd have got a clip round the ear for that one.'

'Oh, she's feisty, all right,' said Seoras, almost deadpan. Jane elbowed him. 'But I wasn't talking about that side of it. There was a woman who came up to us in the town trying to drag me in for a drink. Jane right there. I mean, she was quite brazen.'

'Really?' said Eamon.

'Dark hair. Long dark hair. Very good looking. Younger, sort of thirties. With piercing eyes. Constantly wanted to get me away from Jane and get me to—'

'More than that,' said Jane suddenly. 'He's out for a walk, and she places herself right in his path. Nothing on.'

'That's not strictly true,' said Seoras. 'She had a thong bottom on.'

'Nothing else. I mean, little hussy or what?' said Jane. 'She's lucky I wasn't there. I'd have scalped her one.'

Eamon was laughing now. 'Oh, I'd pay money to see that,' he said.

'Do you know her?' Seoras asked.

'I think I know who you're talking about. She works at the compound. And, yes, she's quite stunning. I mean, she certainly grabs the eye, but she's got a reputation. Be careful. She's got a reputation for older men.'

'Really?' said Seoras. 'In what way?'

Eamon sat back in his chair, crossing his legs. 'I think she's taken a few of them to the cleaners. Took money off them,' he said seriously.

'She comes again for my Seoras, I'll wring her neck,' said Jane.

'I would give a very wide berth,' said Eamon. 'You especially,' he said, looking at Jane. 'She won't like competition, and on one or two occasions, it hasn't ended well. I remember once there was a bit of a fracas, but she's on the good books of the man who runs the place, works up there. Whatever she does for him—and I'm not saying she does that sort of thing for him—but whatever she does for him, he obviously values it. She's still here, despite approaching a few men, and well, she's a relationship killer.'

'Did she ever approach you?' asked Seoras.

'Yes,' said Eamon. 'Certainly.'

'See,' said Jane. 'It wasn't just your body that attracted her. It's the way she is.'

'I'll have you know, many women look this way,' said Seoras.

'I think you and I are past those days,' said Eamon. He stood up and told them to come with him. 'If you want,' he said, 'you can stay the night here. I've got the guest quarters. It's not a big boat, but I don't get that many guests. It's nice to talk to people my age.'

'I'll maybe take you up on it some night, but I think tonight we'll head back, if you don't mind,' said Seoras.

'Of course not. It's one of the nice things about being on a boat. You don't have to worry about how much you've drunk. Especially out here.'

He went up to the wheelhouse and steered the boat back in. Seoras jumped off and tied it up to the jetty. They sat and talked for a little while longer, not about much, Eamon mainly rabbiting on about Ireland and the things that he missed. How he could get most of the football on telly. When it came to say goodnight, he shook Seoras's hand. But he gave Jane a cuddle and kissed her on the cheek.

'You two look after each other,' he said. 'Like I said, that young woman, give her a wide berth. She'll be up to no good, whatever it is. But I will see you around. And don't be shy about coming and asking for me here on the boat. Want another meal? Not a problem.'

'Maybe we'll cook for you,' said Jane.

'I'd appreciate that,' he said. 'I really would.'

They strolled back arm in arm to their hut and once inside, Jane made her way to the bathroom, where she decided to have a shower. Seoras sat down on the bed, taking stock of the evening. As he walked into the shower room, Jane shouted from behind the shower curtain. 'None of that, I'm going to sleep,' she said.

'No, I was going to ask, what did you think of him?'

'He seems nice enough. One of those men. Complimentary. Cheeky with it. Quite like that in him. You know? Probably doesn't sit as well nowadays. Did back in the day though. He would have been seen as a charmer.'

'You think he was playing a role though? Told us to stay away from her. Is that to make sure we find out about her? Is he working for them, is he?'

'I don't think so,' said Jane. 'But then again, all I want to do is go to bed.'

'You relaxed tonight, though. That was good. You needed that. You needed to let it out.'

The shower was turned off, and Jane stepped out, grabbing a towel, and dried herself. She wrapped the towel around herself and then walked over to Seoras, putting her arms around him.

'They shot him. I'm convinced they shot him.' She looked up, and her eyes had tears in them. 'I've tried not to think about it. I try not to let the scene go through my head, but it keeps coming back, Seoras. It keeps coming back.'

He kissed her on the forehead. 'It will do, and when we get out of here, I will get you help, but we have to get out of here first.'

Seoras led her to the bed, where she quickly changed into her nightwear. He climbed in behind her, having changed into his, and held her in the dark. He could hear the odd sniffle, and he told her just to let it go whenever it struck.

Chapter 12

The next morning, Seoras let Jane sleep, leaving a note for her, and grabbed his fedora to head into town. The morning was cooler than it had been, but he made his way to the coffee shop to sit and ponder what to do.

He needed a spade to dig the grave. He wouldn't dig the grave until nighttime, because during the day, with the helicopter and other things about, he could be seen easily. At night, he'd have more of a chance, although he'd have to check the place out. There needed to be no one about.

He thought about buying a spade. But if he did, they would know he'd bought one. He couldn't trust anyone here, could he? The people who worked on the island, they may be working for the man who owned it. They may have a connection. And if suddenly they thought Seoras had a spade, well then, he'd be going to dig with it. You didn't buy a spade on holiday, not unless you bought a bucket with it when you were making sandcastles. And he was too old for that. He sipped his coffee. He thought about what he could do.

Rolling along the street was a Jeep. As it passed by, Seoras could see a small, foldable spade attached to the rear. It parked up at a store a few doors down from him, and something grew in his mind. He couldn't just walk there and take it, could he?

That would be a bad idea, too exposed; he'd be seen to take it. He didn't like the idea of theft either, but needs must.

He finished his coffee, stood up, and walked along to the rear of the Jeep. The owner had gone inside the shop and still hadn't come out. There were several people about. Seoras walked past the Jeep, scanning how the spade was attached. He then made his way back a couple of minutes later, having seen the tie strap that was pulled across holding the spade in place. As he walked past, he reached out and carefully loosened it. The spade almost clattered to the ground, but hung precariously.

He walked a little further down, stood at one of the shops, glancing through some clothing, and then saw the driver come out to get into the Jeep. He drove off, and about fifty yards up the road, the spade fell off the back of the Jeep. Seoras walked along the street, looking to see if anyone had noticed. He bent down, picked up the spade, and then spun about, heading back towards his hut. The spade wasn't large, but it would be enough.

Seoras just needed to get down. He didn't need to exhume the whole body. He just needed to know there's a body in there, if indeed there was. When he arrived back, Jane was up, and she stood looking at the spade.

'What do we do?' she said. 'Do we head out now?'

'No,' said Seoras, 'we go tonight, through the night, so you're going to have to rest up. We'll go to bed separately,' he said. 'I'll go to bed this afternoon and sleep in. You sleep in the early evening, and then we go out together. We need to be awake for this, and we need to be careful. I can't go on my own, in case we get seen. I need somebody on watch while I dig.'

'I could dig if you want.'

'No,' said Seoras. 'I know what things look like, how they

should look when it comes to things like this. It comes from my work. You just have to keep an eye out.'

'Okay,' said Jane.

During the day, Seoras slept and when he woke up, he went and sat outside while Jane slept. While he was doing so, Eamon visited. Seoras offered him a seat outside, telling him that Jane was asleep and was feeling a little under the weather. Eamon had joked it wasn't his food that had done it, but Seoras said no. He was sure that she'd be fine the next day. Eamon stayed for an hour or two before disappearing and giving Seoras more to think about.

He mentioned the woman again, and Seoras wondered why. He'd already told him. By the time it came to late evening, Jane was back up and they dressed. This time, Seoras pulled out as many dark things as he could find, which wasn't easy because Jane had redone his wardrobe. When you went looking for sun and fun, you didn't come away with a night camouflage outfit. But he found a pair of darker trousers, a darker t-shirt. He placed his hat on his head.

Jane was wrapped up in a black shawl and tracksuit bottoms. It was a reasonable hike, and Seoras made sure nobody saw them leave the villa. By the time they were out in the scrubland, he was fairly convinced no one knew they were there. At one point they stopped, as he heard a Jeep nearby, but it went along one of the roads and kept going. After an hour, they came up to the graveyard. Seoras made Jane hunker down while he got closer, looking to see if there was anyone there, but he could see no one. So, carefully, he took the spade, went over to the grave and began to dig. Jane was positioned a short distance away, down in the hollow, but looking all around.

As he dug into the ground, Seoras could feel himself beginning to sweat. He hadn't done something like this in a long time, and the arms and back soon screamed at him. And yet he was trying not to get agitated, not to be annoyed with his body. He needed to stay quiet, needed to do this professionally.

Seoras laughed at himself. *He needed to professionally undig* a grave. Who ever professionally undug graves? When was that skill popping up on his radar?

The spade went in at where Seoras thought the head of anybody would be. There was a thing about laying bodies in and if they placed a headstone there, the head would be towards that end. It was natural. It's what people did, of course. That was if they just put it in with nothing else. They might be zipped up in a bag. He'd have to find out.

He stopped several times to take on some water, because although the night was cooler than the day, it certainly wasn't cold. The darker clothing was also his traveling clothes from earlier in the trip. They weren't really suitable to this island climate. They were, however, dark. Fortunately, the moon was obscured at times by clouds floating past, and Seoras felt he wasn't being watched.

He kept digging down, and he reckoned he was a good foot down now, at least. And suddenly, the spade hit something. He reached down, his hands in the dark, feeling a bag. It was a bag he recognised. He'd seen too many of them in his career. Zipped up, moved off, taken to forensics for examination.

Seoras grimaced, and then he froze. He could hear a sound. Quickly, he put the shovel inside the small hole, covering it up. He was going to kick some soil over, but he heard something and scrambled back over towards the hollow where Jane was. As he got in, she went to speak, and Seoras clapped his hand over her mouth. He pointed, and together they both peered over the top of the hollow.

He saw a guard approach and walk around the grave. It was hard to see, and he wasn't using a torch, which meant the guard was looking for somebody. You would switch off a torch, as it would scare people off. No, this was a quiet check. This was somebody expecting maybe to see someone.

The guard walked right past the hole Seoras had dug. He didn't look at it. Seoras hadn't caused a great disturbance digging as he was in one place, working. The guard was trying to scan around, probably wary that somebody might jump out. There was a voice beyond him, and he turned back to another guard who Seoras could see in the distance. And then they both bolted. They ran off. Jane went to scramble up, but Seoras held her down.

'It could be a trap. We wait, okay? We wait.'

He could hear a vehicle driving off in the distance. And then there was nothing except for the sound of the sea in the distance. There was then a cry from far off. Seoras wondered what was going on, but he didn't care, told Jane to remain where she was and keep a lookout.

He ran back and put his hand down the hole again, feeling the bag that was there. Seoras took the spade and filled in the hole. Rather than compacting it down, he used his bare hands to scrabble the soil over the top. When he was done, he folded the spade and waved at Jane to follow him.

The walk back was done quickly but in absolute silence. Only here and there did Seoras point where to go. Arriving back at the accommodation, Seoras first checked to see if anybody was watching it before they entered quickly. He went to the bathroom, washed his hands, took his clothes off and then washed them in the sink before hanging them up in the bathroom.

Jane had changed into her nightwear, and soon they were both lying in bed. It was close to four in the morning, and they felt like they needed sleep, but neither did. Instead, Jane spoke.

'Was it an old grave?' she asked.

'There may have been a grave there once, but now it's a fresh grave.'

'Is that because of the soil?'

'Well, the soil shows it was covered up recently, but when I put my hand in, I could feel a body bag. I know what a body bag is, know what they feel like. I've worked with them for long enough, and that one down there, that's a modern body bag.'

'Modern? What do you mean by modern?'

'They used to have rubber ones. If that man was buried sixty years ago, they would have had rubber ones. That's a modern body bag. And with how the soil is, I think somebody is buried there. I believe you saw somebody being shot, and they want to know whether you saw it or not. They killed that man. Eamon says that they do chemicals up there. Maybe they do, maybe they don't, who would know? Maybe there's a front there where the chemicals are shipped off, but maybe there's something else going on.'

'So, what do we do?'

'Shush,' said Seoras. He suddenly got out of bed and walked over to the window. He could see Eamon in the distance, walking towards his boat.

'What's Eamon doing up at this time?' he asked out loud.

'Eamon? Eamon's out there?'

'Eamon's out there.'

A vehicle drove past, and Seoras could see two guards in it.

Soon, more guards drove past. Somebody was then outside their front door looking in, and Seoras retreated into bed.

'Lie down,' he said to her. 'Lie down and make as if you're asleep.'

He thought he saw somebody through one of the windows in the hut despite the blinds being down. They couldn't quite keep everybody outside from looking in. If people really wanted to, they could find an angle, He hoped they would find an angle of him lying there in bed beside Jane. He felt her shiver and shake, and he pulled her close.

'Easy. Look like you're asleep. You have to look like—'

'Do you think they followed us?' she whispered.

'No, no, I don't, but I'm wondering what Eamon was doing out there. Go to sleep,' he said. 'It's the best thing we can do at the moment.'

It was another five minutes before he heard a vehicle pulling away, and Seoras thought they'd disappeared. The one advantage they had at the moment was no one knew what Jane knew. They didn't know what she had or hadn't seen, but for some reason it was obviously easier to do nothing if she hadn't seen things.

There was a problem. They were on an island. He was not with his police force back home, for he'd have gone straight into work, straight in to tell them what was happening, and from there, he would get the team out. He would have lifted that grave completely. Yes, he would have had to go through all the proper channels to do it, but he would have done it. Here, he had to work with the evidence he had.

He hadn't seen the face, but somebody, he was sure of it, had been killed. He needed to know who. If he could find out the who, he'd find out the why. And then maybe he could find out who his enemies were in this and who were the good guys. Because at some point he would need help. He was too far from home. Too far away from those he knew. Jane wasn't the only one who was afraid.

Chapter 13

I t was seven in the morning, and Seoras was sitting up in bed. He'd hoped to get more sleep. Whether the fact he'd slept the day before in the late afternoon was a factor, or whether it was just the nervous tension running through his body, he couldn't sleep right now. He watched the woman beside him as she dozed.

He wanted to get Jane out of here as quickly as possible, but he just wasn't sure how. They were trapped. If he wanted a flight out of here, he had to go via the airport, and surely these people would know if he was going from there. He had no other boats to jump onto. Who did he trust? Eamon? And if Eamon wasn't nefarious, he would put Eamon in danger too. And as a policeman, or a former policeman, he couldn't do that.

There was also the call of the chase. He'd said he'd left it all behind, but you never truly leave it all behind. In his heart, he was a detective. He sought justice. He needed to find out what had happened, and to bring those who had done wrong to account. Someone had been shot dead.

He didn't know why, but he wanted to find out why. Wanted, in his core, to know who had done it, and to hold them up to the light. He looked down at Jane. Normally, when he was a detective chief inspector, Jane wasn't involved in any of the cases. There had been times, yes, when being his partner had put her in danger. But those times were rarer, and only when he was attacked personally.

Now, she was the subject. Jane was the one under threat. For if she had seen what she thought she had seen, then they would take her out and him with her.

Jane stirred and rolled over, bumping into Seoras as he sat up in bed. Her arms went around him, pulling tight into his waist. He felt a kiss on the side of his body.

'Why are you awake?' she asked.

'Same reason you are. Scared.'

She slowly lifted herself up until she too was sitting upright, and then leaned back into him, letting his arm go around her.

'I never thought you got scared,' she said.

'Being afraid's good. As long as you can control it. As long as you can think through it. Keeps you sharp. Keeps you doing what you need to do. Can't be without your fears. They help drive certain parts of you.'

'Shush,' she said. 'I don't need an explanation. What are we going to do, though?'

'I don't know. I'm not sure about the status of the island. It seems privately owned, in which case it's difficult to go to the authorities because the authorities look like they're the ones who've done this. There's no police force that I've seen, just these security guards. Again, they seem to work for the person who owns the island. It's awkward, to say the least. In the past, I could always go to my own authority. When I worked abroad, even there, you had authorities to go to. There were people you could turn to who would understand right and wrong. They had the power to arrest people, to bring them in for questioning. We don't have that here. We've got me. My instincts, and you.'

'Me?' said Jane.

'You are good with people. You helped me by being a lookout. It's you and me; we're all we've got here.'

'What was Eamon doing out last night?'

'I don't know,' said Seoras. 'I don't know, but something happened last night. Those guards left. I don't think they watched us last night go up to the grave. I believe if they had, they'd be here, taking us away now. Rather, I think they were patrolling around it. And then they got chased off somewhere. Noises sent them running.'

'What could that have been?'

'I don't know. Is there something else going on? Something more? I don't want to jump to conclusions,' said Seoras. 'There's something more than just a guy getting shot. Why would you shoot him? Why here? Why away from everywhere? What is there?'

'What do we do today, though?' asked Jane

'Well, this morning, we take it easy. We act as if we're on holiday. Maybe we'll go down to the beach again. Maybe we'll sit out front. I'm going to get up and go for a coffee.'

'How? I'm shattered. I mean, we've been up half the night,' said Jane.

'Exactly,' said Seoras. 'So, we get up early and we get coffee, like people who haven't been up half the night.'

She gave him a kiss. 'Well, I'm getting in the shower first, then.'

He watched as she walked over to the shower. While she smiled at him when she saw him looking, when her face turned away, he could almost sense the nervousness in her. He showered after she had, and they dressed in their colourful holiday clothing, walking hand in hand up to the coffee bar. While there, Eamon walked past, giving them a large grin.

'How are you this morning?' he said.

'Fine,' said Seoras. 'Why?'

'Oh, a bit of noise last night. Don't know what went on over on the side of the island, but there were people running around here at five in the morning. Came off the boat to have a look, see what it was. You don't know what it was, do you?'

'Fast asleep,' said Seoras. 'That's what it is to have a woman beside you.'

'True,' said Eamon. 'Don't hire her out, do you?' For a moment, Seoras almost rebuked the comment, but then he saw Eamon's cheeky grin.

'I don't think I can tell her where to go,' said Seoras.

'That's it. That's the one,' said Jane. 'My one-woman man. And he knows it, and he obeys.' They laughed until Eamon was gone, then Jane turned to Seoras. 'So there was some noise last night. Something.'

'Yes,' said Seoras. 'Fortunate that, wasn't it?' But it didn't sound like it was fortunate.

They made their way back to the hut and were about to go down to the beach when a car pulled up outside. Seoras looked through the window and thought it looked like a Rolls-Royce. Strange choice for somewhere like this. The driver got out of the front and opened the rear door. A man dressed in a white suit, with a pristine white shirt underneath, and a red carnation in his suit breast pocket. He looked to be close to Seoras's age. As he came to the door, Seoras recognised him.

'Mr Wainwright, how are you? You didn't need to visit. Have

we done something wrong?'

'No, not at all. Just here to check up on your good lady.'

'She's fine. You really shouldn't have bothered coming out to see her.'

Jane appeared behind Seoras. 'Oh, hello,' she said.

'Hello again, Jane. I was just telling your good man here that I've come round to see how you are.'

'I'm fine. Really, really, I'm fine. Your people keep coming and asking how I am and lots of other stuff, but I'm actually fine. I remember nothing about it, but other than that, I'm fine.'

'Well, that's good. Although you are looking a little peaky, if I may say so.'

'I don't feel peaky. We've just been down for a coffee, and we had an okay night's sleep. There was some noise, though. I've been sleeping better. I think the sunstroke knocked me out for a couple of days, but . . .'

'Are you sure?' he asked.

'Do you want to come in?' asked Seoras. 'Let me get you a coffee or something.'

'No. I don't wish to bother you like that,' said Wainwright. 'Do you have got plans for today?'

'Well, yes,' said Seoras. 'We were going to go out and sit on the beach. We came here for some sun, relaxation, and that. And your island—it's lovely.'

'And oh, the fruit,' said Jane. 'The fruit's fantastic. I've been along nearly every day to get more and more of it. I can't get enough. It's terrific. And I'm managing the heat, now. I like my walks, but I think that was the problem.'

'Sounds like you overdid it when you went on your walk.'

'That must be it,' said Seoras.

'But like I say, I'm feeling absolutely fine now,' said Jane.

'Well, obviously it's your decision, but I think it would be wise to avail yourself of our medical facilities again.'

'Well, if anything else happens, I mean, obviously, I will. We just want to get on with having our holiday now, though.'

'Excellent. Well, you know, I hope that goes well for you, but if there's anything else, do say to us?' He stopped for a moment and thought. 'Tell you what,' said Wainwright, 'why don't you come up to the house? I'm having a party this evening. I don't know if you're into art?'

'No, I'm not,' said Seoras. 'You probably have more idea than I would, Jane. It's all above me, but—'

'Well, there'll be plenty of people there. You can meet some classier people, and I bet if I could explain a bit of the artwork to you, you could get to understand it a bit and enjoy it. I would just feel better if I knew you were enjoying your time. Come up and let me treat you to our art delights.'

'I don't deserve that,' said Jane. 'I just got a bit of sunstroke, nothing more. You don't have to go out of your way like that.'

'No, it's my island and you are visitors here, guests, so please come up here. You seem the type. We have a lot of younger people here who wouldn't appreciate it, running around in the sand. But you look a bit more cultured, if you don't mind me saying so.'

'Well, it's my first time being called cultured,' said Jane.

'We'll come,' said Seoras suddenly. 'Yes, we'll come. It's very kind of you. Decent of you, sir. Thank you very much, Mr Wainwright.'

'Marcus. Call me Marcus. You're on holiday. You're our guests. Do you want me to send a car round for you this evening?'

'You don't have to do that.'

'Well, it makes sense. You could try to get yourself a lift. Taxis here are funny. There's not that many of them. Yes, I'll send a car around for you. Eight o'clock. Would that do?'

'I need something to wear,' said Jane.

'Well, clothes would be preferable,' said Marcus, and then laughed. 'But not too fancy. I mean, this is an island. We don't do overly smart.'

Seoras looked at him. 'You're dressed in a white suit with a little carnation on the side. It looks kind of smart to me.'

'Don't worry, I'm sure we can find something here,' said Jane.

'Tell them to put it on my tab. Tell them Marcus said to charge it to me. Get yourself something at the local shops, okay? And then I'll see you up there tonight. The car will be here at eight o'clock. I look forward to seeing you.'

Marcus extended his hand, and Seoras shook it. 'Excellent,' said Seoras, 'and we'll have a nice quiet day here. And then we'll see you tonight. Thank you again. It's most kind.'

'Not at all,' said Marcus. Seoras stood at the door, watching the man, as the driver opened the car door for him. Marcus got inside and gave a brief wave. As they pulled away, Seoras shut the door behind him. Jane looked up.

'Why did you say we'd go?'

'Why is he here?' asked Seoras.

'Well, he wants to know what I saw.'

'Exactly. Why? Why is *he* here? Complete change of tack. We've got no way of finding out what's going on except through people like him,' said Seoras. 'If we try to get an early plane, they'll come for us. Or, we sit and wait it out. But I don't think they'll let us leave here unless they're convinced that you've seen nothing. So, we play along with it. If we keep refusing,

115

they'll wonder why.'

'We should just get out. Get back to the UK.'

'I thought about that. Can't do it. There's no boat to go. And if we went on a boat, they'd catch up with us. There's a lot of ocean between us and home. Or between any decent country. And I can't sail that far. And what do we do? Grab somebody like Eamon and drop him in it. And that's if he isn't somebody else. If he isn't part of them, playing along.'

'It's the best way. Keep the idea that you've seen nothing, that you just collapsed and you know nothing. And while that's the case, they're not tearing us off into a room somewhere to beat it out of us. Instead, they're trying to cajole and play us along. See if we break down.'

'So, what do we do?' asked Jane.

'Well, this afternoon, we get some new outfits. We look smart and at eight o'clock, we go up and we see what they want to try to get out of us. I will also try to find out more about our island governor, because that's the important bit.'

'Why don't you send some information back home?' asked Jane.

'Because we're on their internet connection. They'll see it. I'm not clever enough to cover that up. Besides, we sent no messages when we arrived. It wasn't like I was in contact with Hope or Clarissa or any other of my former colleagues, having a chat. And then suddenly I send a message? Even if we code it, it's going to look weird.'

'Have you thought about Kirsten?' asked Jane.

'Yes,' said Seoras. Kirsten was a secret agent and former colleague of Seoras's. He took her from being a detective constable to getting her the job in the Secret Service. She was someone who could step in here, who could operate in the dark and in plain sight. But communicating with her would be difficult, and she was thousands of miles away.

If he phoned her, using a number he had on a SIM card she had given him, would it be seen by Wainwright's people? Mobile connections must go through something on the island. He needed another way of communicating.

'We're okay at the moment,' he said to Jane. 'We'll play it this way, see how tonight goes, and then work out what we need to do. But if things get too ropey, we'll call it quits and run. But we need to know how to run, what escape plan could work. I'm afraid that's not something I'm used to.'

Chapter 14

J ane and Seoras made their way into Port's Bay and found
a tailor's shop where Seoras was measured for a suit. He
didn't want to go for a full white one and instead took a
light beige-coloured one. Jane was kitted out in a dress that
hid all the bits that at her age she didn't want seen, and showed
off everything that she did. It matched perfectly with her hair,
and Seoras was stunned when he saw her in it.

The clothes were packed up, handed to them in bags, and
they then went for a coffee. They spent the rest of the day
casually wandering around, but Seoras was deep in thought.

One of his greatest difficulties at the moment was trusting
people, where to go, and how to make it natural. How not
to be forced into what he saw as a dangerous and awkward
situation. Eamon, for example—could they trust him? Was he
working for the governor? If he wasn't, how would he react if
they told him they were party to viewing a killing? Maybe he
would just scarper. Maybe he would drop them in it. People
reacted differently, and until you knew them, you had to be
careful.

That evening as they dressed, and then waited for the car to
arrive, Seoras could see the nerves in Jane. He took her hands.

'Just be yourself when we go. You know what I'm like; I'm quiet, reserved. You're the person who talks to people. Talk to people. Take a genuine interest and just ask things. Don't ask about what you've seen or go too deep into what's done. Ask about the artwork. Ask about their interest in the artwork. Make it normal.'

'You've got a lifetime of doing that.'

'Yes,' said Seoras, 'and that's the thing. You haven't. So just be yourself. Cover nothing up and just be yourself. You'll be fabulous.'

He kissed her on the forehead, and she held him tight. Then there was a rap on the door. Seoras answered it and found a car waiting. He escorted Jane out to the car where a driver held the door open. As they made the journey across the island, Seoras asked the driver,

'How long have you been working for Mr Wainwright?'

'A few years now.'

'That's good.'

'The man's generous.'

'We were quite surprised he came down to see us,' said Seoras. 'It's too much, really. I mean, and these outfits.'

'Always like that. Very generous man, my employer. I wouldn't think too ill of him for it. When you've got a bit of money, it makes sense to use it. Brighten other people's days. He was quite concerned when he heard that you'd fallen over, Miss Hislop.'

'Well, we're very appreciative of this,' said Seoras. And then he saw the house they were going to. It was an extensive structure. Grand steps at the front, a large driveway that swung round, but there was security too. The grounds were fenced off to some degree.

'The trouble when you have money,' said the driver, 'is that other people will come to look for you. You get some funny people out here. And we haven't got a proper police force, so that's why Mr Wainwright has his own security.'

'He certainly has that, hasn't he?' said Seoras, looking around at the armed guards. 'But I can understand it.'

The driver parked the car at the bottom of the large steps up to the house and then opened the door for Jane. Seoras took her arm, and together they walked up to the front door, where a man in a butler's outfit opened it to them.

'Ah, the master's been expecting you. Please, please come in.' They entered and were escorted through a grand hall into a grand room.

Seoras wasn't sure if it was a dining area that had its tables removed, because that was the impression it gave, but inside was a vast number of artworks. Milling around the artworks were various people, most dressed well, and there was a buzz in the room. A waiter came up and offered some drinks, Seoras taking an orange juice while Jane took a glass of wine.

'Clarissa would love this,' said Seoras. DI Clarissa Urquhart ran the arts team under Seoras, back when he was a detective chief inspector. She knew her artwork inside out. Her drive and enthusiasm for the artworks were always evident. Seoras took his mobile phone out and asked Jane to stand in front of a few of them.

He took photographs and, looking at some of the guests, he thought there were a few shady-looking customers. As such, he photographed as many of them as possible in the background.

'Clarissa will love this, won't she?' said Jane.

'Absolutely.'

As he stood watching the guests, Seoras could tell who the dodgy characters were. He'd seen Clarissa look at artwork before, for she was a lover of it. She knew where it all came from, and if she didn't, Clarissa hungered to find out. She hungered, but she also stood back and enjoyed it. And that was the difference.

These people looked at the pieces like they were made up of pound signs. What was it worth? Not aesthetically, not in your soul, but in your bank balance. Seoras didn't know his art, but he knew people.

'Aha, you've made it. Delighted to see you here.' It was Marcus Wainwright, and he strolled forward, shaking Seoras by the hand, before then coming up and kissing Jane on either cheek. 'Delighted you can make it. Do you like what you see?'

'I'm not really much of an arts person, so I don't really know what I'm looking at. But yes, it's fantastic.' Jane stepped forward and went to touch one piece of marble. 'How it's cut—it's fabulous, isn't it? It's rather erotic too, though, isn't it?' said Jane.

'Rather, a delicate piece,' said Marcus, 'but you didn't tell me. I believe we have the great DCI Macleod here amongst us.'

'No, you've just got Seoras,' Seoras said. 'I left the detective chief inspector behind a while ago now. I'm just here with Jane. It's the two of us, and I'm retired, and I'm trying to find a bit of fun. We're out in the sun. Jane loves the sun. I like the walking. We're just enjoying what remains of life.'

'You make it sound like we're nearly dead,' said Jane suddenly, causing Marcus to laugh.

'You've quite a way about you, haven't you?' he said to Jane. Jane put her arm out, touching the man on the shoulder.

'This is what he's like. This is what I had to get rid of. You

121

can imagine, if he's being a detective, he is so, so serious. But there's a fun side to him. There really is a fun side to him. Look!'

She put an arm up on the piece of marble and then turned to kiss it. The statue was of a man with nothing on. Seoras took out his phone, capturing a few of the people in the background. He saw the slightly worried look on the governor's face before a smile came across it.

'You really are all one, aren't you?'

'Well, we can't come to something like this and not take some photographs to remember,' said Seoras. 'Maybe everybody will get lined up later on.'

'Well, we'll have to see about other people. I mean, not everyone is as forward as yourself,' said Marcus. 'Maybe they'll want a little bit of privacy. Some people are funny about having their pictures taken. Some of these people are quite rich. They don't like, or are certainly not used to, being ordered about.'

'Well, of course not,' said Jane. 'Sorry. Got a little carried away. Glass of wine too, you know.'

'How about a photograph of you with Jane?' asked Seoras.

'Not now, maybe later. I need to talk to some of the other guests,' said Marcus. He slipped away quietly, leaving Seoras thinking. *He doesn't want a photograph, and yet he's quite happy to say that I've been recognised.*

He took Jane by the arm. 'Come on, round some of the other pieces here.' He whispered, 'I want to get a photograph of everything. Get it to Clarissa.'

Jane posed with everything. Some guests were laughing at her, and she shook hands with them, talking to them, telling why she'd never seen such a thing before. Jane had much more understanding than that, Seoras knew, but she was playing a part. She wasn't being herself. She was being more than herself, quite over the top.

She'd only had a glass or two of wine, and yet she was acting like she was almost plastered. Clever, though. Disarming everybody as Seoras took photographs. But maybe they'd come for the camera later. Maybe they'd do something about that. He'd have to be careful. Jane flung her arm around him, kissing him on the cheek.

'This is James,' she said. 'He's got his own yacht. Apparently, the yacht's nearly bigger than this house. Can you believe that, Seoras? Why would you bother with a house? Do you still have a house as well?' she asked James.

The man smiled. 'Have you had enough to drink yet?'

'No,' said Jane. 'I haven't even begun to have enough to drink. Where's the bar?'

Jane continued to pick up a drink every now and again, but Seoras watched her. She didn't drink that much. Instead, the drink was deposited here and there, dropped into plants. At one point, she was hugging him, telling him she loved him and then she whispered in his ear, 'Am I doing okay?'

'You're doing terrific. Just keep it up.'

Seoras smiled as if there was something wrong with his face, walked around, and shook hands with everyone. He asked some of them about some of the artwork. Nodded sagely as they talked about how much it was worth. But a few of the items, people didn't seem to talk about. And yet, he saw Marcus with a few of them, talking to people. Hands were shaken in a way that looked like a deal, not like a welcome.

At one point, the men disappeared out onto a veranda at the rear of the house. Cigars were handed out, but Seoras shook his head. Marcus came up beside him.

123

'Surely you can allow yourself a cigar.'

'Don't drink, don't smoke,' said Seoras.

'And you were a policeman?'

'Some of us didn't need vices to forget things. Some of us just managed.'

'You're quite famous back in Scotland, aren't you?'

'I'm known from being on the telly,' said Seoras. 'But famous? No, you will not get me on one of those game shows.'

'Some of my people said you're quite smart,' said Marcus.

'Well, I've left the job behind and I'm still sane. I must have been fairly smart.'

'Your wife's quite something.'

'My partner. We didn't get married. I had a wife once. She died quite young.'

'So Jane and you are a recent connection?'

'Well, several years now, but yes, fairly recently. Found each other later in life and realised what we wanted. Takes time sometimes to realise what you want, don't you find?'

'Yes, but you've got to go for it,' said Marcus. 'If you don't go for it, you don't get.'

'Indeed,' said Seoras. 'Quite something you have here though, the island, miles away from everyone. I was talking to a man on a boat, and he said that most of your money was made from the chemicals you make in the plant here.'

'Well, a large part, yes. I don't share my business interests too broadly. You've got to be careful. You know, when you're successful, people want to know. People want to get involved, want to steal your ideas, want to do what you're doing. End up bringing you down. Dog-eat-dog world in a lot of ways.'

'It isn't different when you're a copper,' said Seoras. 'Dog-eat-dog there too. Some people don't like successful policemen.

They don't like them when they look like me.'

'Oh,' said Marcus.

'I had a partner. She was far better looking. They wanted her to be the face of everything.'

'Oh, the redheaded one,' said Marcus. 'Yes, my people showed me something about her.'

'Brilliant detective,' said Seoras, 'but hamstrung by the force because they want her to be the face of it. Detectives aren't there to be the face of something. Detectives are there to solve crimes. It's a pity because she was an outstanding detective.'

'Some words coming from you. They said you solved just about everything.'

'Didn't get them all. Now, I'd better find out where Jane is, see what trouble she's getting herself into.'

The rest of the evening went without incident, and as they were going to the door, Marcus shook their hands. 'I'll get my driver to run you back down,' he said.

'No, no,' said Seoras. 'We'll walk.'

'That's quite a distance.'

'We need to walk for a bit. When Jane gets this much in her, she needs to walk it off. You can't take her back to the house. She'll not sleep properly. We'll walk back and we get to one of the outlying places. Maybe we'll grab a taxi from there. There'll be one about, and I've got the mobile. I can ring one. We want to walk for a bit.'

'No, my man can do that. He'll follow you.'

'No, no. You've done too much for us already, I'm sure. And besides, she likes it. She and I together, walking, you know.'

'I'm walking,' Jane announced as she half stumbled over to Seoras. She came over to Marcus, threw her arms around him, and planted two kisses on his cheek. 'You're a lovely man,' she

125

said. Seoras grabbed her as she went to fall.

'Okay,' said Marcus, 'if you think so, but please do ring, you know, if you get any problems.'

Together they walked off, out of the driveway and estate, out into the dark. There was enough moonlight to follow the road, and several cars passed by, until eventually, after about twenty minutes, they were on their own.

How did I do?' asked Jane.

'Brilliant. You play the part well. Well, I took a lot of photographs. We've got pictures of everybody who was there, and I've got the artworks.'

'You are serious about getting a taxi at some point though, aren't you?' asked Jane. 'I'm not walking all the way back.'

'Yes, that's what we'll do. That's what I said I would do. Keep up the pretence.'

Seoras could hear a car in the distance and helped Jane over to the side of the road. He wasn't bothered, for there were cars and Jeeps driving about at this time of night. Close to midnight, but not so close that you'd be bothered to hear a car. But he heard it reduce speed as it came up behind him, and then it pulled over in front of them. The car stopped, and the driver's door opened.

Chapter 15

Seoras almost hated himself for it, but he recognised the leg that emerged. It was the young woman. As she got out of the car, he saw an incredibly short skirt. She had a loose jacket on, with a light top underneath. Her hair swung behind her as she started striding towards him.

'Come with me,' she said.

'What? I've told you before I'm not interested.'

'You need to come with me. You know you want to come with me.'

The accent was funny. Seoras wasn't sure where she was from, but the woman walked up to him and put an arm on his shoulder and a leg up against him. She grabbed his hand with strength as he tried to pull it back, before placing it at the side of her waist.

'You can get your hands off him,' cried Jane.

'Why?' The woman ran her hand up Seoras' chest and pulled herself in close. 'You come with me; you could come too.'

Seoras didn't quite know what to do. Should he push her off? He was trying to see if she had any sort of weapon. She was being quite forceful, and he could feel a hand moving onto his back. Jane, however, was near exploding. He could see the

127

anger in her eyes, but rather than push the woman away, given where they were in the dark, Seoras continued to look for a weapon.

This wasn't normal behaviour. Certainly, it wasn't the behaviour of a woman who simply wanted sex. And he still couldn't get over the idea that she would want him for any reason other than trying to find out what Jane knew. It was one of the joys of how he looked. He would hardly be sought as a sex object. Although Jane was whipping herself up into such a storm now. He might have to rethink that.

Jane reached forward to grab the woman, but an arm shot out, pushing her backwards, causing Jane to stumble. Seoras went to catch her, but the woman was pulling him in tight, nails raking into his side.

'You come with me,' she said again. Seoras worried that if she had a weapon, she might go for Jane. But Jane was rallying and turning to come at the woman again. As she did so, Seoras could hear another vehicle. It pulled up at the side of the road.

'What's all this then? Walking in the dark? Can I give you a lift?' Eamon's smiling face jumped down from the Jeep, and he marched over. 'Good man yourself, Seoras. It's you out here. How are you? I'll take them from here, love. It's fine. It's not a problem.'

He approached Seoras, grabbed his hand to shake it, and almost physically pulled him out of the way. Eamon positioned himself between Jane and the woman, indicating Jane should get into the Jeep. He pushed Seoras in that direction too, and then kept himself between Jane and the woman as Jane clambered on board.

'You'll get cold out here, love, wearing stuff like that. You get yourself home, all right? Don't be bothering my friends again. They don't like drunks out here. I'll have to talk to the governor if you keep doing this to people. Not good, all right? We'll just say nothing about it. Get my two friends home, okay?'

Eamon started the Jeep and drove off. He kept looking behind him in the rearview mirror until they were a distance away.

'Well, she's not following,' said Eamon. 'I told you about her. Likes men. I think she might be funny in the head.'

'She just jumped me. Pounced on me.'

'Really,' said Eamon. 'I knew she was forward, but that body you hide must be something else. Or is it the deodorant? And in front of you too, Jane. You looked like you were about to take her on.'

'Had a bit too much to drink,' said Jane. Seoras, of course, knew this was a lie, but Jane had picked up her role again. That was good thinking. He didn't know who Eamon was. Any casual comment about Jane's state, needed to be accurate, backed up by her behaviour. Accurate in how the governor thought she had been. Her reaction to the woman was perfect, though it was very genuine. He didn't blame her for that one.

'Where have you been?' said Eamon. 'You're very dressed up to be out walking about.'

'We got invited up to the governor's. He came round, asked how Jane was and then he asked us to come and see some of his art. There was a good number of people there. And he bought us these outfits as well. He must have serious money,' said Seoras.

'Oh, that he does. That he does.'

'He offered us a lift back, but I refused it,' said Seoras.

'That might have been unwise,' said Eamon. 'She's obviously

129

been following you, that woman.'

Seoras nodded, and Eamon drove the Jeep back to their hut. He stopped outside and helped Jane down. She stumbled as Eamon helped her to the front door. Seoras opened it, and once inside, he stopped.

'Would you mind waiting outside for a moment? With Jane, please,' said Seoras.

'Problem?' asked Eamon.

'Somebody's been in here,' said Seoras. 'I'm going to check everywhere. Just stay outside with Jane. Keep her safe.'

'Okay,' said Eamon. 'But shout if you need me.'

Seoras scanned the rooms of the hut. Doors had been opened. Clothes had been moved. Things had been gone through. It was good, not that much disturbed from before, most things put back accurately, but it wasn't that good. Some things had been left in different places.

One thing about being a detective was you got used to seeing changes. And there had been a change in here. He sniffed the air. Seoras thought it might be the woman who had been in. She was usually heavily perfumed, but there was nothing here. Somebody had been in. They were being watched.

The hut had been turned over while they were at the governor's function. And they'd been offered a lift back from the governors. Was that lift going to take them somewhere else? Had the woman been sent then to haul them back in? Why had they been allowed to leave? There were other people there, of course. Easier to be seen to be leaving and then to disappear.

'Are you okay in there?'

'Yes. Yes, Eamon. I'm fine. There's nobody here, but this place has been gone through. Do you think that woman's capable of this?'

'Well, possibly,' said Eamon. 'I mean, you said she just walked up to you tonight. Nutter.'

'Clearly.'

'Why don't you come back to my yacht?' suggested Eamon. 'I've got the guest quarters there. You might feel safer. I mean, just in case she comes back tonight. Maybe you could talk to the governor about her tomorrow.'

'That's an idea,' said Seoras. 'Jane?'

Jane was leaning against a wall, continuing the act of being drunk. 'Yes,' she said.

'Shall we go to Eamon's and sleep on his boat tonight? Somebody's been in here.'

'Get me a bed,' she moaned.

'You take her back to the Jeep, Eamon. Thank you. I'll lock up,' said Seoras. He went through and grabbed their passports and other essential items, packing them in his small case. He put some clothes in for himself and some for Jane, a wash bag, and then joined Eamon in the Jeep. The journey to the jetty was a very short one, and Eamon said nothing until he parked up.

'Did you have problems like this before?'

'What do you mean?'

'You said you were a policeman. Did people harass you before in other places.'

'No, not really. Why do you ask?'

'Well, just in case you were used to it. I'm not. Well, she never came to harass me. Clearly, I don't look the part.'

'He's mine,' said Jane, overhearing them.

'Let's get her to bed,' said Seoras. Eamon helped Jane to the guest room on board the yacht. Once inside, he asked Seoras if he wanted a nightcap, saying that even though he didn't drink, he could make him something nice. Seoras nodded, and when Eamon had left the cabin, he laid Jane down on the bed.

'Get you into bed. Go to sleep. I want to see if I can get any more information out of Eamon. He seems a good egg, but something's wrong. I don't fully trust him. He's not telling me something. The man was probing me then about being a policeman, without asking stuff beyond what he knew. He wanted to, though. I could sense it.'

'Okay,' said Jane, 'but don't leave me tonight. She scared me when she went for you. And when she shoved me, she was forceful.'

'She raked her nails into my back,' said Seoras, pulling up his jacket and then shirt.

'She's drawing blood. That bitch drew blood on you.'

'Easy, easy, you're drunk, remember? Just go to sleep. I've been hurt far worse than that.'

Jane changed and got into bed. Seoras kissed her goodnight before going up to the upper deck, where a glass of a green liquid was waiting for him.

'It's non-alcoholic, don't worry,' said Eamon. Eamon, however, had some sort of whiskey. Seoras sniffed his drink. It was minty. Excellently done.

'Hope you don't mind me saying so,' said Eamon, 'but I haven't heard of anybody having their place gone through here. That woman's been a nutter at times. She's caused havoc. But having their place going through, I've not heard her do that before.'

'I guess there's a first for everything,' said Seoras.

'She seems to have taken a real interest in you. I noticed the medical people around you a lot. Are you okay?'

'Well, we're stopping on your boat tonight, so I guess we're not that okay. And you've been a great help, so thank you for that.'

'There was a bit of commotion the other night,' said Eamon. 'That wasn't you, was it?'

'Commotion? We were in bed. Saw nothing that night.'

'Okay. I didn't want to say this,' said Eamon. 'Certainly, didn't want to say it in front of Jane, but you're a man of the world, a policeman. Somebody doesn't seem to be too happy with you. You may not have been out at something the other night, but they may think you have. I don't know why. I said before some of what they do out there is, well, not abiding by official regulations and all that stuff. So maybe they think you might be looking into them.'

'I'm retired. I'm on holiday.'

'Well, that's a good cover story,' said Eamon. 'And you don't have to tell me if you are or not. I'm just looking out for you. You see, they may think the same about you I'm thinking. I wouldn't want to see you get into trouble if it's wrong.'

'It's certainly been a hassle. Well, I'm grateful for your vigilance in looking out for us, but it's okay. I can handle myself. And no, I'm not here to investigate them. And if they've got that idea—'

'Well, the governor, I think, would have asked you up to check you out. Did he know anything about you?'

'He seemed to know me.'

'I mean, beyond being a policeman. You've told me you're a policeman. I'm sure you've probably mentioned that to somebody else. Did he know what sort of policeman you were? Did he know details about you? Because that's what they'd look into if they thought you were looking into them.'

133

'I know what they would look into. I was a policeman,' said Seoras. 'I really do appreciate what you're doing here, Eamon. And I appreciate the fact that you're letting us stay on board. But there's nothing to see. Whether it's a mistaken identity or it's because they think I'm here to do something I'm not, we'll clear it up. I'll go to see them. We'll sort it out. I don't want you dragged into it, though. You've been so helpful.'

'It's fine, happy to help, you know, at the end of the day, happy to assist someone from back home.'

'We'll see you in the morning,' said Seoras. 'Jane will be sober again, we'll sit and we'll talk about it.'

'Well, don't race off, I'll serve you breakfast here. Won't be a problem, okay? Have a lie-in. If anybody comes to see you where you are, I'll not let on you're here. You can tell them afterwards. Having gone through what you have tonight, it'll be perfectly understandable that you slept elsewhere.'

'Thank you,' said Seoras. He drank the last of his mint liquid. Eamon asked if he wanted another, and Seoras refused. 'I had best get to bed. She'll be nervous. And she's not in her right mind.'

'Of course,' said Eamon. 'I'll keep an eye out up here and make sure nobody's about. If need be, I'll just anchor up further out.'

'Don't do too much,' said Seoras. 'I don't want them thinking that I'm actually hiding something because I'm not.'

'Got you!'

'And thanks again,' he said to Eamon, shaking hands with him. Seoras made his way down to the cabin, got into his pyjamas and climbed in. Jane was still awake.

'Are we worried?' she said.

'I am worried. I'm very worried. Those people tonight—

there's something about those artworks. Why did he bring me up? He's trying to flush us out. He knew I was DCI Macleod. They've done their research about me. Now they're trying to find out what I know. I think they would have taken us from that place tonight, and they would have tried to extract information. Gone back in the car to some room to sweat it out of us. They've searched the hut, but everything we know is in our heads. Nowhere else. We've taken no photographs. The only photographs we have are from the party because we were there. Maybe he's regretting that. Sent his woman out to get us, pull us in. And then Eamon shows up.'

'Is Eamon okay?'

'I don't know,' said Seoras. 'I just don't know about Eamon. He was asking if we were involved in the commotion the other night. He was out and about, though. I just don't know about Eamon.'

'But are we safe here on his boat?'

'We might be safer here.'

'Might be?'

'Might be, Jane. That's all I've got.'

Chapter 16

J ane awoke, and it took her eyes a moment to adjust to where she was. The interior fabric of the cabin was stunning. Mahogany, oak, something like that. She was never good at knowing what wood was what, but the richness of the colours pleased her, and she took a moment to dwell on them.

Beside her, Seoras was lightly snoring, but his hands were still wrapped around her. She didn't move, letting him lie, as she glanced up at the fixtures and fittings. It would be nice to be able to afford something like this. Something like this would suit her. Seoras and her sailing everywhere together. She wasn't sure if she could take this island life forever, though.

To be on a boat out here, is that what she'd want? The sun was nice, but she didn't have a life here; she had a break; she had an excursion. How would you set up a life here? What would you do? There wasn't much going on after all, was there?

Everybody was just getting away from it. Either that or they were scraping a living fishing or probably working up at that plant. She stopped for a moment. The image of the man came to her head again. The head being forced backwards by the shot.

She shouldn't think about it; really shouldn't think about it. She shivered. They were in a tight situation now. She felt the arms around her squeeze a little harder.

'You're up then,' he said.

'Well, you weren't. You were snoring.'

'I don't snore.'

'Yes, you do.'

'Never heard myself snore,' said Seoras. He got an elbow in the ribs for that one.

'What are we doing today?' asked Jane.

'I want to get some of these pictures to Clarissa. The ones at the party.'

'So how do we do it? You said we're going to have to be careful,' said Jane. 'If they operate the mobile signal, they can intercept everything we put up. All the data flows through their station here. Won't it?'

'I don't know; I'm a little stumped, you know. It's not my area of expertise. Ross would usually have dealt with this.'

Ross was Seoras's former sergeant, who'd been an expert on computers and kept him right on everything from Zoom calls to emails and the like.

'I wonder if Eamon's got a satellite connection.'

'What?' asked Seoras.'

'Satellite connection. Maybe he runs all of his Wi-Fi through here; I could find out.'

'What, you're just going to ask him if you can upload some photos?' asked Seoras.

'He likes me.'

'Well, he might sit with you and watch what you're doing.'

'And so what?' said Jane. 'If he did, we're uploading pictures

137

of us at a party. We're not uploading gangster hood shots, you know. There isn't a sign underneath with a name and number.'

'Well, it's up to you, love,' he said. 'I have no idea what I'm doing with it. Oh, Eamon said we would have breakfast here with him, up on deck.'

There was a knock at the door. Seoras pulled the covers up until they covered Jane's neck.

'Come in.'

The door opened, and Eamon was standing in a bathrobe. 'I was just going to do the breakfast. Are you ready to come up soon? I didn't want to wake you too early.'

'We can do breakfast,' said Seoras.

'What have you got?' asked Jane.

'I have some eggs, some scrambled eggs with salmon. Well, it's not salmon. It's a local fish, but it'll be like that,' said Eamon, waving his hand. 'Do you want some Buck's Fizz to start the day? A little hair of the dog?'

'No,' said Jane. 'I'll just take a couple of paracetamol.'

Eamon nodded and closed the door.

'A couple of paracetamol? You're not even drunk.'

'You said get into character. I'm in character. And I'll stay in character, don't worry. We'll see if he can help us get the pictures away. If he can, that will be good.'

The pair got out of bed and put on bathrobes over their pyjamas. Climbing up the decks of the boat, they found Eamon in the galley about to serve up, and he pointed out to the table on the deck.

'Lovely fresh morning,' he said, and it was. A light breeze was blowing as they sat down at the table and Eamon served up their eggs and fish course. Jane woofed it down. She was hungry, starving. Jane always had a good appetite, and although she wasn't some sort of fitness guru, she thought herself reasonably trim for her years. She could get about, and that surely was the whole point.

Seoras has always had a slimmer figure. It's just the way he's built. Not massively tall, but elegant. Not really a Scotsman in some ways, Jane thought. *Maybe one of those thinner ones.*

She wondered, did they differ from the Highlands to the Lowlands? There were some Scotsmen with wide, broad shoulders, thick, tree-trunk-like legs, and they suited a kilt. She didn't think Seoras would look good in a kilt. He'd certainly never asked to be in one.

'So, you slept well, did you?' asked Eamon.

'Yes, thank you.'

'I haven't noticed any more movement over by your hut. I get a bit of a view from here.'

Seoras looked over, and Jane, following his eyes, could see their hut and how easy it was to spot what was going on around it.

'It's a bit of a funny one,' said Eamon, 'coming and searching the place. Sounds crazy. Maybe you should stay here for a while, might be better. If there's any trouble we can just let the boat go, head out into the ocean away from everything.'

'It won't be that sort of trouble, will it?' asked Seoras. Jane hoped not, but she very much thought there might be. She knew Seoras didn't fully trust Eamon.

'I think we'll head back to our accommodation now. It's better to face this head-on. If that woman comes back, well, I'm going to go to the governor and just tell him.'

'Just be careful. She works for him. You never quite know how people are with each other, you know. In any trouble, come and see me. I've got the gift of the gab. I can usually sort things out.'

'Well, that's very kind of you. And you've been more than kind,' said Seoras.

'Absolutely,' said Jane. They finished breakfast and Seoras disappeared down below to their cabin to have a shower. Jane sat opposite Eamon.

'If he ever isn't enough for you,' said Eamon.

'Don't start that again. I don't mind polite buttering up, but that's my man, okay?'

'Pity,' said Eamon. 'You enjoy your eggs?'

'You know how to cook, don't you? You're not shabby with it.'

'Plenty of time to learn when you're out here on your own?'

'Speaking of that,' said Jane, 'I was hoping to get hold of some papers, but I guess they don't arrive here until about three or four days after, do they? If they get here at all.'

'No, they don't.'

'I can get them online, but I seem to be having a bit of trouble with the internet provided by the island. I don't want to give them a load of hassle with everything else that's going on, just for a look at some papers. You don't have an internet connection yourself?'

Eamon pointed up to the top of the boat. 'That's the satellite connection. Would you like to use it?'

'Oh, that would be terrific. Thank you. Thank you very much.'

'Well, hang on a minute,' he said. 'I'll just get you the code.'

Eamon disappeared off and then came back with a small piece of paper, which he placed in front of Jane. She clicked on the indicated router and then typed in a code and found that her internet worked perfectly.

'I think this will do it,' she said. 'Spot on.'

It was about ten minutes later when Seoras came back up. His hair was wet, and he had changed from the suit he'd worn the night before into some clothing that he'd brought in the small case. She hadn't seen him pack it.

'There are clothes for you down there, too. I picked them out, but don't shout at me. It was last night. You were very drunk.'

'You see, Eamon, this is why I'm with him. He's such a star, thinking of me.'

Jane disappeared down below deck and could hear Seoras talking to Eamon. Once inside the cabin, she put an email together, sending it to Clarissa. She attached all the photographs she'd taken and asked Clarissa if she saw anything there of interest. She didn't want to put too much into the email in case Eamon, or any of his people, whoever they may be, intercepted it. Jane hoped he was the good Samaritan he was portraying.

She pressed send and watched as the message disappeared before jumping out of her bathrobe and into the shower. She stood washing her hair under the water, fighting to keep that image away again. Seoras had said she would get help when she got home. Jane hoped so, for she was going to need it.

She realised she was completely stressed. Her body felt knackered, exhausted. It was the constant worry, the hanging threat that somebody might lift them, interrogate them, or do worse. That's what Seoras had said, wasn't it? Interrogation never sounded good. It sounded painful. She never could believe how Seoras could stay so calm in these situations. He was like a rock, never moving, never flinching.

Jane wondered what the job had done to him over the years. He was a warm enough man, especially with her. She

141

wondered if part of him was cold. Was that how you survived? He'd seen bodies before, people killed. He'd seen children die. She couldn't take that. Not kids. There's something wrong in a child dying.

She hopped out of the shower, dried, and changed into the clothes Seoras had packed. The top and bottoms did not match. That was Seoras, clueless, clueless about any sort of fashion. She was no fashion guru herself, but she knew what colour went with what.

She checked the phone, but there was no reply. Of course, Clarissa would probably be asleep at the moment for she was on the other side of the world. That was the other problem, wasn't it? How did she get the reply? Seoras has said they were going to leave the boat. What was she meant to do? Pop up and say, no, we're not leaving the boat. I need to get online to read the papers.

She brushed her hair, made herself look presentable, and then went back up on deck. 'What's your plan?' asked Eamon of Seoras as Jane approached him.

'Well, I don't know. Do we go out and fish? Crabbing was good before. Might keep us out of the hair of people.'

'That's a good idea,' said Eamonn. 'Head out. In fact, why don't we just take this boat and head out? You could fish off of it. It's not a problem.'

'We don't want to get in your way, cause you hassle,' said Seoras.

'You can't cause me hassle. I don't do anything. Like I told you, I've got a pot of money coming in. I can just sit back and spend the day fishing.'

'No,' said Seoras. 'No. We'd be taking up too much of your time.'

'Well, tell you what,' said Eamon. 'Why don't you leave your stuff here? And then tonight, if you've had any more bother, you can come straight back. It's not a problem. If not, you can come and fetch the rest of your clothing and take it back to the hut.'

'That's a good idea,' said Seoras. 'I agree with that one.' Seoras and Jane went down below and Seoras made sure that their passports were tucked away on Eamon's boat.

'You trust him then?' asked Jane.

'I trust that he's not part of Marcus Wainwright's crew. He's definitely independent, whatever he's doing. I'm not sure what, though.'

When they came back up on deck, Jane looked down, saw the young couple who had run around starkers and pointed them out to Eamon. 'Those two. They went straight past us on the beach in the buff. Unbelievable.'

'Wow. That's quite something, isn't it?' said Eamon. 'Did you enjoy the view?'

Jane hit him. 'Don't be crude.'

'At my age, there's no shame left.'

'You're not old. You're no older than me,' said Jane, giving the man a tap on the arm again. 'Got to think young. Think about being wonderful at our age.'

'Think about the legs, think about the joints, more like,' said Seoras.

'I'm going to get a younger man. You two are rubbish,' said Jane. They laughed, and she followed Seoras down onto the jetty, waving goodbye to Eamon.

Making their way back to the hut, they entered, and Seoras determined that the place hadn't been turned over again. Once they were inside, Jane's shoulders slumped.

143

'I keep seeing it,' she said. 'Keep seeing them shoot him. I'm doing my best to keep a jovial face out there. I try not to think of it, but it keeps coming back.'

Seoras put his arms around her. 'It will, and I know, I know it's difficult. But you have to keep going. We'll get away today. We'll do something else, I think.'

'You're not worried they'll just come and pick us up?'

'It's a game we're playing. It's a game on the edge. They will not come and pick us up. Not here; too open. They need to find a way of us disappearing like it's our fault. They could do that in the night, nobody about, everybody asleep, come in, kidnap us, take us away. To do it during the day is tough.'

'But how long do we play this?'

'We haven't got a choice,' said Seoras. 'If Clarissa comes back with some information, we might make a different move. You've got your phone on you?'

'No,' said Jane. 'I left it deliberately on his boat. It's of no use to me here, is it? After all, if I catch up to the internet, they might see her reply coming back to me. I left it on the boat. Make sure we go back there today.'

'And all we've got to do is work out what to do today. I think we'll keep our heads down,' said Seoras.

'Let's get out of the way. Somewhere I can stop pretending for a bit.'

'I'll go book a boat. Let's go fishing,' Seoras said. And she smiled back at him.

Chapter 17

'Done it,' said Seoras, coming in the door and putting his fedora hat down to one side. 'I've hired a small boat to go fishing. I said we'd be back there in about an hour.'

'An hour? I'm ready to go now,' said Jane.

'Well, let's go and have a coffee, and then we'll go. It takes time for them to get it ready.'

'Is that what they said to you?'

'It was hired out yesterday. He's just cleaning it through. It's the same one we hired before.'

'OK. Make sure I take some sunscreen as well. It's always warmer out on the water. Maybe we'll get some fruit too. Make a day of it when we're out there. I mean, that's what to do, isn't it? Act normal.'

'Act normal,' said Seoras.

The pair walked into town and sat down for coffee. When they'd finished, they went along to various stores, picking up fruit and meat for sandwiches, and then headed to collect their hire boat. Seoras took the boat out of the small harbour and around the side of the island.

This time they went to the opposite side of the island from

where they'd been before. Seoras didn't want to provoke a reaction. He also didn't go too far from shore, making sure that they could be seen at all times. There were other sea users about—people on paddle boards, canoeists, others in their boats and on their jet skis. It wasn't the best place to go fishing because of the noise, but Seoras didn't care. They were out in the open, hard to be grabbed without people noticing.

'Are you feeling any better being out here?' asked Seoras.

'No, I'll be better when I'm out of here—when I'm away.'

'You need to wind down before that,' said Seoras. 'If you don't, you'll exhaust yourself, and if big moments come, you won't be able to handle them.'

'What sort of big moments?'

'I don't know what's coming,' said Seoras, 'but it's coming.'

He sat back in his chair, fishing rod resting up against the edge of the boat and the line out into the water. He took his hat and placed it across his face, looking like he was snoozing. It kept the sun off and that was important out here. He could hear Jane moving about, fidgeting.

'You have to relax. Wind down. You can't keep going like this. I couldn't do it when I was investigating. If you were intense the whole time, you were exhausted after about twelve hours.'

'Well, crack me a joke then, Mr Comedian,' said Jane. 'Excuse me, it's my first time being hunted down by people. It's my first killing.'

'Sorry,' he said. 'I guess I just take it for granted. I mean, that's what I was involved in. Mostly, I never told you about the different hairy situations we got into.'

'Why not?'

'Because you were at home and you did not need to worry

about me being out and about. That was one of the key things. The dangers that went with the police work. If you knew them, what would be the point? You would just worry. And you couldn't do anything to solve them. So, I never told you half of them. Uh-oh,' said Seoras suddenly, lifting his hat. 'Do you see who I see?'

A small boat with an outboard motor went past him. In a tiny bikini was the woman who had accosted Seoras before. She grinned at him as her boat went across the bow of his. She didn't go very far away before she stopped her boat and put on a snorkelling mask and some diving gear.

'Interesting, eh?' muttered Seoras.

Another boat pulled up on the other side of them, and this time they recognised the young couple. When they stopped their boat, the couple jumped off the deck and frolicked together in the sea.

Jane was looking over the side at them, and Seoras rebuked her. 'Don't watch,' he said.

'It's just my jealousy. I mean, you and I could jump in there.'

'We could. I'd be back out of there pretty quickly. I don't care what they say about how warm the sea is here; it's not that warm to me.'

'You wouldn't stay in it if a good-looking woman like me was in there?'

'Course I would,' he said, and he reached to trap her behind, but she spun round, right behind him first, and hugged him. 'Wished I had known you when you were younger.'

'No, you don't. I was a stickler. A religious nut job.'

'I've never heard you call them religious nut jobs.'

'Well, I can say what I want now,' Seoras grinned. 'I'm finding that no longer being a detective chief inspector, the mouth works a lot quicker. I don't know if that's a good or a bad thing.'

'Well, as long as you keep the talk to me nice and lively, I don't care,' she said. 'You can tell me whatever you want; you know that, don't you? Especially if it's about interesting things with me.'

'You're outrageous,' he said. 'But I might just do that.'

He felt a hand go down underneath his top and run across his chest. 'Promises,' she said. 'That's just promises. I need delivery. I need—' Suddenly, the boat felt like it was moving slightly, listing to one side.

'What on earth's that?' asked Jane.

'I don't know.'

Seoras was out of his chair and down below deck. He looked across towards the bow, where there was a large amount of water pouring in. It wasn't just pouring in. The boat was tipping down towards it. He saw an almighty hole punctured in the bow. No, was that sawed? Drilled? What was that?

But he didn't have time. The boat was starting to coup, and he fought to get back up and onto deck again. Jane was shouting at him, from up above as he tried to climb back up. As the vessel couped, Jane fell forward, past Seoras into the rapidly increasing water below.

She was now underwater inside the cabin. Quickly, he tried to dive to grab her. But as he got his head under the water, he could see no movement from her, as if she were unconscious. He tried to reach for her, but then an arm grabbed him and pulled him up. As he broke the surface of the water, but still inside the boat, he saw the young woman who had been frolicking with her partner. Beyond her was her partner, who continued to pull Seoras upward.

He tried to shout, tell them that Jane was down there, and he saw the young woman disappear downwards. Then he was being pulled away, hauled off the boat, into the sea beyond, and then across to the small boat belonging to the couple. He was pushed up and rolled onto the small deck.

Seoras tried to lift himself up onto his feet, but he couldn't. But on his knees, he came to the side of the boat, looking for Jane. The hire boat was now three quarters of the way gone, sinking rapidly. He watched as it disappeared down beneath the waves, his heart sinking. Then, a little distance away, a head he was very familiar with broke the surface.

Her hair was soaking wet, and she was being dragged along through the water by the young woman. As they got near to the boat, the young woman pushed Jane up, and she rolled into the middle of the deck. The young man pushed Seoras aside and began checking her breath. Jane started to cough and spit water. She looked groggy, unsure of where she was. Seoras grabbed her hand.

'It's okay, it's okay. Is she all right?' he asked the young man, 'Is she okay?'

The young woman was now getting on board, coughing and spluttering. But the young man was working away at Jane. He went for towels, came back and wrapped them around her. Seoras was then handed a silver blanket, which he put around him. He looked around for the woman, the one who had accosted him, but her boat was gone.

Had she seriously sunk him? Had they looked to kill him that way? Well, it would have been a tragedy, but an explainable one. A good way to get rid of them. But then the people at the boatyard, did they know? The hull had been breached properly. She'd gone along with something and cut into it.

'I don't know how well she is. You need to get checked over,' said the young man. 'We'll get you back to land. We'll get you to the medical centre.'

No, thought Seoras. *I am not going to that medical centre. I can't take her there.* He looked around, wondering what to do.

'Look,' said the young man. 'I'm not a doctor. She's come round, but she was unconscious.'

The young woman looked over at Seoras. 'She was out cold. She needs checked. She can't just walk off after this.'

'Yes, you have to get looked at,' said the young man.

They turned to take them back to shore but a larger vessel suddenly came across the bow and stopped.

'Does anybody need a hand? I heard a boat was going down.'

'This man here, his boat sank. I was just going to take his wife to the medical centre.'

'Seoras,' Eamon shouted from his own boat. 'Seoras, what on earth? Is she okay?'

'She needs to go to the medical centre. She's not right,' said the young woman. 'Was out cold. She's recovering now, but she was unconscious.'

'Transfer them onto my boat. I can deal with it. It's a larger boat, be easier to handle if she's not in immediate danger and just needs checked.'

'I can take her straight in,' said the young man on the boat.

'No,' said Seoras. 'Go to the other boat. He's got some of our things. It'll be all right with him. That's Eamon. He's a friend.'

They pulled the boat up alongside Eamon's, and Jane was lifted by the three men onto the boat. Seoras turned and shook the hands of the young man and woman.

'You want me to go and report it?' asked the young man. 'Tell him the boat's gone down.'

'I'll do that,' said Eamon. 'Don't worry about that. You two just get back to enjoying whatever you were doing. And thank you. You've been a great help.'

Seoras looked over at them, nodded his thanks, but his eyes returned to Jane. Eamon spun the boat around and powered back towards his berth at the jetty. But instead of going in, he moored up just a little way out.

Eamon came over to Jane, but first he picked up a bag and placed it beside her. He removed from it various bits of medical equipment, including a stethoscope and a light to look into eyes and ears. He gave her the once-over.

'Follow my finger,' he said, watching her closely.

'Is she fine? Is she okay? Do you—?' started Seoras.

'I've had some training as a doctor in the past. Well, medic, more of a first-aid medic. I think she's okay. She seems to be, but we'll monitor her in the next twenty-four hours. Must have been a heck of a shock for the pair of you.'

'It was. But I think somebody sank the boat,' said Seoras.

'You what?' said Eamon.

'Somebody sank the boat. When I went down below, there was a large hole. There's nothing to hit out there. There were no rocks I could see.'

'There are no rocks in the charts either,' said Eamon. 'That's the cleanest bit of sea you're ever going to have over there. So, I don't know what happened to your boat. Maybe it failed structurally.'

Seoras sat down, almost brooding over what had happened. But Jane was getting up on her feet now.

'Are you okay?' asked Eamon.

'I think so,' she said. 'I reached down for Seoras. The boat had tilted and I reached for Seoras, and I just fell in. I think I hit my head on the way down. And then I was under the water. But I was out. I must have been under the water because that's the way I was going before I blacked out. And the next thing I knew, I was up here, well not here—on another boat, a small boat. Where's that gone?'

'Two people rescued you; I've brought you on board here.'

'It was the two young people, the ones running around starkers, those two,' said Seoras. 'But that woman was near our boat.'

'What woman? You mean . . . not the one?' said Eamon.

'Yes, that one. The one that accosted me, the one that probably turned the house over, the one who—'

'Well, I don't want to tell you what to do,' said Eamonn, 'but if I were you, I'd stay on my boat. It seems that, for some reason, you've upset people. You've certainly upset her. Maybe you've upset Mr Wainwright as well. Either way, I think you should keep it quiet, stay here.'

'I think you're right,' said Seoras. 'What about Jane?'

'I think the best thing for Jane, in my limited medical training, is that she go downstairs and gets some rest. I'll monitor her, popping down every twenty minutes.'

Together, they helped Jane to her feet, and Seoras walked her down the steps until they found her cabin again. Once inside, he helped her change into pyjamas and then tucked her up in bed.

'Good job they were there,' said Jane suddenly.

'It is, isn't it? That's the second time, at least, that somebody's come to our rescue.'

'How do you mean?' said Jane.

'Well, Eamon came when that woman went nuts at us. Now we've got a hole in the boat, and our two frolicking friends have helped us out. And then Eamon's there too.'

'You think it's all too good to be true?'

'I'm thinking there's something else going on here. Something more. Something deeper. I don't know what. But I'll go up and I'll talk to him and see what I can pry out of him. You get sleep. I don't think Eamon's malicious. I think he's looking to protect you. So, if he says, get some sleep, I think getting sleep would be a good idea.'

Jane nodded, and Seoras stood in the doorway for a moment before climbing back up to the decks.

'Well, there's no commotion, considering a boat's just gone down. I thought people would be out to investigate, but there's nothing.'

'Thank you,' said Seoras.

'For what?' asked Eamon.

'You were just in the vicinity, were you? You just popped round? I think you were watching our boat today.'

'Well, I was just in the vicinity,' said Eamon, deadpan.

'Either way. Thank you. Without our two younger friends and yourself, there'd be no conversation here. Jane and I would be down in the depths of that sea.'

'Well, what's friends for, eh? Call me a friend. Well, friends are here to look after and protect, and don't you forget it. Anyway, stay on board until you work out what you want to do. I'll keep Jane safe, and I'll probably give her as good medical care as you can get without going to the centre.'

'You're very kind.'

'No,' said Eamonn, 'just doing the right thing.'

Chapter 18

J ane lay in the comfortable bed of the cabin on Eamon's yacht. It was palatial, with comfort all around, but Jane was restless. Seoras and Eamon had insisted that she stay there, that she rest up, for they said she'd blacked out, gone under for a while, but she felt fine.

She had banged her head. That was all. She could feel where the bump was now, but she was fine. Nonetheless, if she stepped out of that cabin, they would have hit the roof. One of Seoras's worst faults was that he was too protective. She didn't need protecting.

Well, that wasn't true. She needed protecting at times, and she needed protecting when she was on this island. But sometimes, with little things like this, a bang on the head, he could go too far. He never really understood the medical side of things. He never understood what was bad and what wasn't. And therefore, took the ridiculously large precaution of just stopping you from doing anything. *It could be worse*, she thought.

She heard the vibration of her phone, which she'd left in the cabin when they'd previously left Eamon's yacht. She picked up the phone and found a video message from Clarissa. When she pressed play, she could hear Frank, Clarissa's partner, talking as well as Clarissa.

They were looking at some of the pictures which Jane had sent Clarissa. The video was showing them discussing the images. There were moments of Clarissa talking about what something was, and then Frank would intercede, explaining that she was wrong and it was this or it was that.

Jane found that rather amusing because Frank knew nothing about art, certainly not like Clarissa did. As far as Jane was aware, the man golfed. He looked after the greens and fairways. They then mentioned some of the people. Clarissa was also speaking in a rather jovial tone. She pointed at one man and mentioned about his hackney roots, how he looks like someone who came off the back of a boat somewhere, ended up in the UK, and then started dealing.

It wasn't like her. At least, it wasn't the Clarissa that Jane thought of. Frank was coming in with some ludicrous comments as well. And everything was like a big laugh. Jane didn't know what to make of it. She closed down the phone, placed it to one side and rolled out of bed.

She found a bathrobe, put it on, and then opened the bedroom door before making her way up the stairs to the deck outside. Seoras was sitting, fedora adorning his head, on the sofa where they'd talked the previous night. But it was Eamon who noticed her first

'Whoa, easy,' he said, racing over to her and putting a protective arm around her. 'You need to be careful. You've had a—'

'I'm fine. Would you leave me alone?' said Jane. And then she halted. 'Sorry, it wasn't meant to be that rude, but I'm fine. I can walk on my own. I'm good.'

'Okay,' said Eamon. 'I mean, if you know best . . .'

'I do,' snapped Jane.

'I think you should go back to bed. You can't just bounce up from these things,' said Seoras. 'Doctors would have you—'

'Doctors, what do they know!' And then Jane thought suddenly. She made a half pitch forward, causing Eamon to start.

'Whoa, whoa, you need to head back. I'll take you back down,' said Eamon.

'No, no, let Seoras take me. You've done enough. I'll head back down. Seoras, come on, give me a hand.' Seoras came over and put an arm around her for support. Together, they made their way down the stairs. He opened the cabin door, and once inside, with the door closed behind them, Jane shook him off.

'I'm fine, I'm fine, I manufactured that stumble.'

'Why?' asked Seoras.

'Because I needed to get you down here without him coming.'

'Why, what's up?'

'I got a message back from Clarissa, but it's weird.'

'What do you mean it's weird?'

'It's not like Clarissa at all. Frank's in it. Why is Frank in a message?'

'Because it's a video, you know people do videos nowadays. Send video messages; we don't just tap—phones have moved on.'

'I know phones have moved on.' That caused Jane to laugh. She'd seen Seoras trying to work a phone; he wasn't good, and the simpler they were, the better for him.

Before he'd left the police force, Ross had programmed several buttons on the front of his smartphones that Seoras simply pressed to get through to certain applications and back to other people. That was the limit of his using a phone; now he was out of the service. Ross had kindly equipped his phone, but he didn't see Ross every day and therefore, he was losing the knowledge. Still he had her. He didn't need to be on his phone all day.

'Watch this,' she said. She picked up the phone, sat down on the bed and tapped the covers so he would sit down beside her. She then played him the clip.

'What's she up to?' said Seoras.

'Exactly. That's what I was thinking. What is she at? Look at what she's doing. Clarissa doesn't talk like that. She doesn't laugh at people. She doesn't.'

She saw Seoras's face suddenly tighten. 'Shush,' he said. 'Start from the beginning and shush.'

'Don't shush me. Just ask me to be quiet. You don't shush me.'

'Be quiet then, please, but play it from the start.'

Jane played it and sat watching Seoras' face. He gave a brief nod every now and again. 'What?' said Jane.

'Shush, it's still playing. I told you.'

'You don't shush me.'

'Well, shush woman, I'm listening.'

Jane held her tongue this time and waited until it was over. Seoras sat back suddenly, and she could see he was thinking. Best not to interrupt him when he was thinking. His mind would grind away, and if you talked to him, you got nothing, not truly. You might get a polite comment back; she was more likely to get a shush. But when he was ready, he'd start again, and he'd tell her all that he'd found out. She waited patiently, but then.

'Play it again,' he said.

'Why, what is it?'

'Just play it again.'

'Is that what you would have told Hope? If your sergeant or inspector said to you, what are you thinking? You would have just told them to shush, told them to wait, told them to—'

'Not now,' said Seoras. 'Shush, play it.'

She didn't grind her teeth, but she played the video. She sat in silence until it was finished again. Then he stood up and paced in the cabin.

'What?' she asked.

'I need to think. I need to—'

'Why? What has it got you thinking? What is—'

He sat down. 'Sorry. Look, they're talking there, and it's been prepped. Clarissa's prepped this. Everything Frank says is complete nonsense, okay? Frank's just there to throw other people off the trail. What Clarissa says, even though the way she says it is not good, is accurate. At least, that's what I'm thinking. She says several of them are dealers, but not good dealers. Dealers in artwork. Stolen artworks. She says how different ones are in different countries. People have come from different places. One of them comes to the UK. The one at the back of the room came to the UK from another country, picked up the art livelihood there. Interestingly, she talks about the governor. Did you hear what she said about him?'

'Mr Bigwig,' said Jane.

'Yes, Mr Bigwig, the one in charge. Somebody who's pulling it all in. She's telling us we're in with some big-time art thieves and dealers. And of those works, she's indicated, at least one or two of them are stolen. She's obviously not going to be able to tell that about all of them. She probably can't get close enough with some of them. But she's telling me who they are and what the items are, in a general sense. And she's telling me we're in trouble.'

'Well, what should we do?' asked Jane.

'We need to leave. We need to leave,' he said.

'Shouldn't you arrest them or something, though?' asked Jane.

'How?' said Seoras. 'I have no powers here. It's not even a UK protectorate or part of the glorious old empire. It's an island that we've got nothing to do with. We are visitors. What am I meant to do? How am I meant to arrest them? There's no police force here. There are just the security guards. And who runs the security guards? Mr Wainwright. Mr Bigwig,' said Seoras.

'So, what do we do?' asked Jane.

'One plan would have been to stay here, have a normal rest of the holiday and then just get on a flight and go. Act as if nothing had happened. But I don't think they're going to let us do that. So, we need to get out. We either sail out or fly out. I can't fly a plane, nor can you. So that will not happen.'

'What about a boat?' asked Jane. 'We can ask Eamon to take us.'

'We still don't know who Eamon is. Eamon could be anybody.'

'He doesn't seem to work for them,' said Jane. 'After all, he rescued us from that stupid woman.'

'He did. But why? Was that a ruse to get us in here, to get our confidence, where we would talk more openly to him? Share what was happening? I mean, if we're asking him to get us out of here, we're confirming to him that something's

159

happened. You've seen something, and maybe then he'll act. Or maybe he's working for a different side, maybe he has a vested interest, or maybe he's just a random person who we then bring in. And then what? He drops us off, and they go after him to get to us.

'I'm not prepared to do that. I'm not prepared to bring other people in and risk them when they're not actually involved. If he's what he purports to be, then we would put him at a substantial risk, and if he isn't, who knows what will stir up, or how it will stir it up. We'd be better off getting a boat of our own, but to sail it so far? That would be awkward. The best bet might even be that couple, the ones who fished us out of the water.'

'Why?' asked Jane.

'Well, they didn't let us die. Somebody sabotaged the boat to get rid of us, but they saved us. So, they're not on that side. That's an enormous risk to take if you needed us alive, but they don't. Why would they need us alive? All we can tell them is whether you saw something, and if you did, well then they'd have to kill us again. It makes no sense. Those two are almost definitely a good bet but whether they would help us is unknown. And once again we're bringing in people and putting them at risk. We need to get the authorities in. Some sort of authority, but who?'

'How do we do that?' asked Jane. 'Is there an emergency number? Can we contact the British consulate? Can we—'

'With what? You thought you saw something. I found a body bag. I haven't found a body,' he said. 'At the moment, there's a lot of circumstantial evidence, but there's no body. You want to say somebody's died, show them a body. Who is it? Who do they belong to? What country? Why would the UK bother about coming here if the person who's died isn't even a UK citizen and it's on foreign soil? They might come and get us out. But there again, we'd have to present them with things. It's a big risk to run, interfering in another country. And this piece of land must be owned by somebody, beyond the private owner. There must be a country attached to it, surely.'

'So, you're saying we're stuck? We have got no way out.'

'If we can find out who the person is, and they're a citizen of a country, I can present a dead body to that country. One of your citizens has been killed. That might bias their intervention.'

'So how do we do that?'

'I need to dig up the body,' said Seoras. 'I need to dig up the body, get a photograph, get him identified. Also, we might get some of Wainwright's artworks identified. Maybe they've been taken from someone.'

'Well, Clarissa could do that, surely.'

'If she could be sure, she'd have said so on the video. She'd have showed that to me. Clarissa might even have given a country, people who were stolen from. She hasn't. I think her difficulty is that she's not close enough. It's not a simple thing to identify fakes and that. But she believes these things are real and she said some of them were stolen in her coded way. The other problem we have then,' said Seoras, 'is getting them to believe us when we're on the island and sending things in via phone.'

'So, you want to dig up the body?' said Jane.

'And we stay here. We stay here on Eamon's boat because at the moment it feels like safe land. In the middle of the night, we'll find that body. Photograph it. If the body's been moved since, well then, we're snookered. We just flee, somehow, anyhow, to a safe country. Get home.'

161

'So, what do I do?' she said.

'You come with me,' said Seoras. 'I don't want you left on your own. I don't—'

'This is not about you protecting me. I mean, you're going to take me to dig up a body with all those guards about. You're taking me into the danger area. Clearly, it's safer to be on the boat,' said Jane.

'Yes. But you'll be with me. I'll be able to—.'

'Seoras, let's get something straight here. I don't need protected by you. Well, I do. But not in that way. I need to go with you to help you. You're going to need a lookout, going to need somebody to be there. You can't dig and watch all around you. And you'll probably need somebody to operate the phone just to take a photograph.'

He gave a wry smile at that one. 'So basically, you're agreeing with me,' he said. 'Just for a different reason. But you're agreeing you need to come.'

'Yes, I do. But for now, I'll lie down here in bed and pretend I'm not feeling great. That'll work best then. At nighttime, it means you won't have to stay up late talking to Eamon. You can look after me, and then we can watch for him going to bed. Then we get off the boat and do our digging.'

'Well, you better head back up,' she said. 'Keep Eamon company. We'll do it tonight. If Clarissa sends anything else, I'll work out a way of getting hold of you.'

'You'll be coming up for lunch. ' It won't be that difficult,' said Seoras. He turned and kissed her on the forehead. 'I'll get you out. Don't worry.'

'Don't tell me not to worry when you're worried,' she said. 'I can tell. This is me you're talking to. You're not leading a team here. It's us.'

'I know,' he said and kissed her forehead again. She watched as Seoras stood up, opened the cabin door and looked back at her briefly before closing it. She could see it in his eyes. He was trying to stay calm, trying to give her reassurance, trying to let her know he could manage this, but behind that mask he was really struggling. No wonder, she thought, he normally has his arms and legs, his team around him, but his arms and legs are no longer with him. It's just that brain. She hoped that would be enough.

Chapter 19

Chapter 19

Seoras sat back on the sofa with one of the non-alcoholic mint drinks that Eamon was constantly feeding him. It seemed to do him good. They were cool; they were refreshing, and he couldn't notice any side effects from them. He watched Eamon as the man went about his business on the boat before sitting down with a large whiskey.

He asked after Jane, and Seoras said she was okay, but sometimes she needed to be told to look after herself. Eamon nodded.

'You're okay to stay here as long as you want, you know that. I mean, clearly there are things going on here that aren't right. If that woman is still pestering you, you're safe here. I can keep her off the boat. It's a great pity though, because, you know, you're away on your first holiday, was it? I think Jane said that the other night.'

'Well, first actual break since I retired,' said Seoras. 'We were on holiday before; we were on a cruise ship.' He thought about that one. People had died on the cruise ship, so it hadn't been much of a holiday.

'Did you enjoy that one?' asked Eamon.

Enjoy? thought Seoras. *Actually, I enjoyed that one. I was on a case.*

'Yes, it was fine. Just out there among the waves. These cruise ships are something else. They've got so much entertainment for you. Things to do.'

'What's it like being a policeman? I mean, what rank did you get to?'

Seoras remembered that he'd been called out as DCI Macleod by Wainwright. So, he thought it best not to lie, just in case Eamon was batting for the same side. 'Detective Chief Inspector before I retired. Spent a long time, though, as a detective inspector. That was the place to be, at the coalface. Once I got bumped up to DCI, it was too much paperwork. Too much filling in of forms, checking budgets and that.'

'So why did you move up?' asked Eamon.

'Got out of the way of a young one coming up behind me.'

'Who was that?'

'Hope McGrath. She was my sergeant at one point when I was a detective inspector and then she moved up when I moved up. Well, I got out of the way for her. She had a child, and I'm his godfather.'

'You like that term, godfather.'

'It doesn't really sit with a DCI,' said Seoras. 'Not when you think what godfather means. Well, in the movie sense.'

Eamon laughed. 'He's got you to keep him on the straight and narrow.' And then the man was up on his feet, over to the side of his boat, looking down towards the jetty. 'Oh aye,' he said. 'Rolls-Royce down there.'

Seoras flinched. Wainwright had come in a Rolls-Royce. Was he seeking them again? Why? What was he up to now?

'It's the governor,' said Eamon. 'The governor's coming to

visit you. My, my, this must be getting serious.' He put his hand out and waved down at the car.

'Come board. Would you like a drink, sir?'

Seoras remained sitting, and eventually the governor arrived up on the top deck to be handed a large whisky by Eamon.

'Please, please, sit down. You know my guest, don't you?' said Eamon.

'DCI Macleod, I just thought I should come and find you. I hear you had a bit of trouble the other night. I've had a word with that woman. She's not stable.'

'See, I told you,' said Eamon. 'She's not stable at all. It's all right, Governor. I sorted them out. They've been staying here. I think she went into his accommodation and turned it over.'

'Really? Is that true?' asked the Governor.

'Somebody did,' said Seoras. 'Somebody had been inside and somebody had gone through our things. Eamon here was kind enough to let us use his guest cabin.'

'Well, that's not on,' said the governor. 'I insist you must come up and stay with me up at the house.'

'No, that's too much, far too much,' said Seoras. 'Eamon here has been very generous, and as you can see, it's quite some yacht.'

'But you'll have much more room with me. We have a chef as well. We would—'

'It's fine,' said Eamon. 'They're great company for me. There's just myself and the boat. There's—'

'I won't hear of it,' said the governor. 'Come on, get your belongings.'

'We can't go at the moment anyway,' said Seoras. 'Jane's recovering. We had a slight accident with one of the boats.'

'An accident? I hadn't heard about that.'

'Well, I don't know what happened yesterday. Hole in the boat. The boat sank, and we got hauled to safety.'

Seoras watched the man's face. There was a brief delay. Just a momentary delay. And then the flicker of shock. He had read millions of faces in his police work, and you had to be good to get past Seoras Macleod. Unfortunately for the governor, he wasn't.

'That's shocking,' said the governor. 'Well, I insist, I absolutely must bring you up and get you to the medical centre. Get you to—'

'I have everything covered,' said Eamon. 'To be honest, it's not a problem. I'm enjoying the company, and I have a bit of a medical background. Jane's fine; she just needs some rest. It's very gracious of you, but really, we're fine here. If Seoras wants to stay, it's not a problem.'

'We're down here beside everything,' said Seoras to the governor. 'Up at your house, we'd have to run back and forward.'

'My driver will take you back and forward. Wherever you need to go, it's not a problem,' he said. 'Really, I must insist.'

'And I'm insisting that Jane doesn't move for a while,' said Seoras. 'The boat is good here. It's letting us relax. Very kind of you, but I must say no. For her health, obviously.'

'Well, if that's the way it is, I must insist Eamon takes some funding from me for looking after our guests, won't you?'

'I want nothing,' Eamon said. 'On the house; they're a great company.'

'Well, if you need anything, don't hesitate to ask,' said the governor, stepping forward. Seoras stood up and shook his hand.

'Thanks for coming out,' he said. 'Appreciate it.'

'Well, I hope you have a better rest of your stay. I can't believe it's gone this bad for you. So many things. Terrible, terrible. Well, I'll sort it out for you.' He walked away, down the stairs, towards the jetty.

Eamon turned to look at Seoras, who simply raised his shoulders, but his face creased when Eamon turned away. *Coming to us, putting us up there, but Eamonn didn't give us up.*

Eamonn's face was different from the governor's. Seoras had seen many a face, and Eamonn was hiding something, but he was also very intense in defending Seoras. There was a protective side to what Eamonn was doing, though Seoras didn't know why. Eamonn and the governor were not on the same side. There was definitely something between them. He'd have to find out what.

How to get away, how to get out of this situation would depend on reading people. Seoras was used to evidence, used to churning up facts and details, used to getting hold of people and sweating them in interview rooms or out at crime scenes. This was different. He had his wits, his eyes, his ears, listening to words, judging people. He had no forensics to produce unseen details. It was all about his feel and judgement.

Eamon provided another excellent dinner, but Seoras had said they needed an early night, and so by ten o'clock Seoras and Jane were in their cabin. They sat in silence, listening quietly. After an hour of complete quiet, Seoras opened the cabin door. He crept down the corridor but then thought he could hear the radio inside Eamon's own cabin. He returned, and the pair dressed in the darkest clothes they had. Seoras made sure to pop his fedora onto his head. Jane and Seoras made their way quietly off the boat.

There were others about in the town, but they stayed in the

shadows and then raced over to their own accommodation. Seoras picked up the spade from his baggage and together they vanished off into the scrubland. Keeping away from the paths, they traversed over towards the graveyard, arriving and finding the hollow again, where Seoras made them sit down.

He listened intently but couldn't hear anyone. Seoras briefed Jane again on how to be a lookout, what to listen for, and what sounds to make if there was trouble. Having done this, he opened up the spade and walked over to the grave. He worked as quickly as he could, lifting the soil to one side. He'd need to extract a whole body, and for that, Jane would have to help lift it out.

As the soil came away, Seoras worked along the length of what would be the body. After an hour, he'd lifted enough of the shallow grave away that he could see the entire body bag.

It was definitely a modern one. He got down on his knees and pulled back the zipper, yanking it open, and then recoiling from the stench. The body inside was certainly deceased, and there was a certain smell to it having been wrapped up inside the bag. But it hadn't decomposed badly.

Seoras dropped the spade and hurried over, getting Jane's phone. He raced back, telling Jane to stay in the hollow so she wouldn't have to look at the body. He took pictures of it. It took him a moment or two to operate the phone in the dark, and he even set off the flash by accident. It was then that he heard the noise.

'Oh yes, oh yes, yes,' came the shout.

What on earth? he thought. *Sounds like a couple. It sounds like, well . . .*

Then there were footsteps, thundering footsteps, people running. He looked down. There was no way he could

169

cover the grave now. No way! He ran the zipper up, closing over the face that had stoically looked back at him. Seoras had ignored the sight, ignored the hole in the head. He had methodically taken the photographs but as he went to turn away, the murdered man's face suddenly made him feel his stomach go tight.

This was a dead body, abandoned. He forced himself to turn away.

Grabbing the spade and heading off to the hollow, there were more shouts and shrieks. A woman's cry in the air. A shout of 'come on, run!' as he peered out over the hollow. Holding Jane's hand, he could see plenty of guards. Then he saw a man and a woman running. They seemed to wear very little, and the guards were after them. The guards, however, were spread wide, and the ones on the edge were now coming past the graveyard, and the uncovered shallow grave.

One guard spotted it and moved over towards it. Seoras looked around. There was only one direction out; the couple chased by the guards had prevented them from going that way. But that would have been up towards the facility. He couldn't walk back towards where the grave was because of the guard now looking down at the body bag.

He grabbed Jane's hand and ran out the other side of the hollow, into the dark, away from everything. What would he do now? The body had been found. The body had been found uncovered. He dropped the shovel behind him. They would know it was him, know he had seen it. They'd come now! Could he go to Eamon and tell Eamon to do . . . what? Just sail away?

Sailing wasn't the greatest option. You could be caught up. Eamon had a boat, and it was a good boat, but there were always faster craft. He needed time to think, to know what to do. Behind him, Jane kept looking back.

'Forward, keep looking forward, keep looking forward,' Seoras said. Those behind us would have come for us by now if they'd seen us.'

'Okay,' said Jane breathlessly. 'Okay.'

'We need cover, cover for the night. We need somewhere just to hide out.' As he ran, he realised they were getting close to the roadside. Looking over, he could see a man in a Jeep.

'Is that?'

'Yes,' said Jane. 'It's Eamon. We could go to Eamon, we could go for Eamon's boat, we could get away.'

'No, it's too risky. Too risky,' said Seoras. 'We could put him in danger as well, or he could end up handing us to them. I still don't know who he is, what he's doing, why he's helping us.'

Seoras pulled Jane off in a different direction. As he looked back, he saw Eamon watching them. They were heading now to the opposite side of the island, away from where Jane had seen the man being shot. Away from the graveyard, over towards some of the tiny villages. 'We need to hide, and we can't hide in the open when daylight comes. We need to get inside somewhere,' said Seoras.

'Then let's go,' Jane urged. His heart thumped. He shook. Never had such terror run through him in all his days. Terror for her as much as for himself. Seoras had put himself at risk before. That was never a problem. But Jane was with him, and he had to keep her safe. She may have been his partner. She may have been the one helping him with this investigation of sorts. But she was also the only thing in this life that he truly loved. Above almost everything else, he had to keep her safe.

171

And that was why the terror was getting hold of him.

Chapter 20

J ane awoke to the smell of a pig not that far away from her, and there was only a small barrier between her and it. The creature was penned in, along with a couple of others. Seoras had found them a bed of straw up the side of the small shed where the pigs lived. The stench was powerful, but they'd slept through the night, and now as she awoke, she was glad his arms were still around her.

'Are you awake yet?' she whispered into the darkness. There was light leaking through the sides. It was a complicated run for the pigs to get out, but that made the interior particularly dark.

'Better wait for a while,' said Seoras. 'Our friends haven't been too noisy, anyway. They seem to have accepted that we're lying over on this side, but we'll need to move at some point. You don't build an interior section in a pig house unless you've got a reason for coming in this side. Somebody will come in here during the day. Anyway, we can't hole up here forever.'

'I don't really want to,' said Jane, and almost choked as a few feet away, a pig deposited on the ground. 'This would be funny if it wasn't for the seriousness of it.'

'I know you wanted to show me the world,' said Seoras, 'but

I'm not sure I wanted to see this side of it.'

She knew he was trying to lift her spirits, to keep them both buoyed. The night had been awkward, to say the least. She could tell that Seoras had been bothered by seeing the man. He hadn't shown her the photograph, telling her she'd no need to see it. But clearly, it hadn't been a pleasant image.

'How do we get to the authorities then?' asked Jane. 'We have the photograph, so who do we go to with it?'

'I don't think it's going to be enough,' said Seoras.

'What do you mean?' asked Jane.

'They'll move the body now they know we've seen it. They also know that you saw something because I wouldn't be running after a body if you hadn't. So, from now on, we are totally on the run. We'll have difficulty in trusting anyone.'

'But we could get him identified. We could find out who he is,' said Jane. 'You could contact Hope or one of them to get an ID on the man. They could find him, couldn't they?'

'We could do. We'd have to send it by phone, though.'

'If we got him identified, we could get that country to come.'

'I don't know. I don't know what law exists here,' said Seoras. 'We're not in the UK. We're out on our own. It's the equivalent of the Wild West out here, I guess.'

'But there must be some links. After all, tourists from the UK come here. We did.'

'No, you went off-piste, as ever. You didn't go on a nice package holiday. We're out here in a place that's very different from where most people go. We're not in the Seychelles but a private island, a part of the world that may have different rules. That's why I'm currently lying in a pigsty.'

'So, what do we do?'

'Well, your idea of getting the photo of the man sent back is a good one.'

'We need the internet for that, Seoras. We can't send it via their internet. Maybe we should get back onto Eamon's boat.'

'They'll be watching Eamon's boat if Eamon isn't involved with them. That's a place they'll look for us. They may even turn up and harass the man, for all we know. But he was out there last night,' said Seoras. 'Eamon was out watching us.'

'Why would he do that?' asked Jane.

'He must have heard us get off the boat. I think Eamon is somebody else.'

'What do you mean?'

'Last night, think about it. I was there digging. There was the body, but there were lots of guards about. They weren't that far away, and then suddenly they're off chasing that young couple. I assume it was that young streaking couple. They were certainly a young couple. We got rescued by that young couple from the boat as well.'

'We could search up the man's face, find out who he is, find out if he's associated with anything,' said Jane. 'I can do that on a computer. I'm not as illiterate on a computer as you are.'

'Most people aren't,' said Seoras. 'But if we're going to do that, as you said, we can't use any of the island connections with our phone.'

'No,' said Jane. 'But we could use a fixed station. Use a fixed station that belongs to the island. They won't be looking on there. They'll be looking for our phone, our connections.'

'Where would we go, though?' asked Seoras. 'Where would be the easiest to access?'

'Well, somewhere private. Somewhere where people use a computer and don't want to be disturbed. But also somewhere we know. We don't want to go somewhere that we don't know, do we?'

'No,' said Seoras. 'Because if people come, we've got to get away; we want to be seen by as few people as possible.'

'Medical centre, then. We've been in the medical centre, been in and about it,' said Jane. 'Doctors will use their computers without other people being in the room, deliberately. We could jump one of the doctors, tie them up and then use—'

'Whoa,' said Seoras. 'Jump one of the doctors? We're not the Secret Service here, okay? I was a detective chief inspector. I had teams of uniforms who could go in and kick down doors and do the rough stuff if I needed them to. But generally, I didn't. I didn't run around like a 1970s' copper. We're not in a TV movie here.'

'So what?'

'So we sneak. We stay quiet. We don't give ourselves away as much as possible. The other thing we need to look at are the art items. We need to get a better idea of what they are. Clarissa indicated they're valuable, or that there were possibly stolen items amongst them. We need to get into the governor's house and get a better idea of what has been stolen and what hasn't. If items are particularly hot, he's not going to have shown them to us. The items that were there must have been hard for me to identify, even to think about.'

'Right, he'll have checked and made sure that you didn't know your art before calling us up to the house. Or maybe that was a test to see if you'd react. Maybe that was why you were going to be picked up afterwards by that woman. Maybe it was all part of their plan to do that.'

'I don't know,' said Seoras. 'But if we can find stolen items in there, we could go to their owners. They might come for them. That could be a ticket out. But we'd have to find the owners.'

'It would be insane trying to get back in there,' said Jane

'We're running out of options,' said Seoras. 'I can't be a Kirsten. I can't be a secret service agent like she is. I can't grab a weapon, beat people up, or bring the whole thing down. We've got to use what we're good at. That's my brain, and that's your abilities on the computers. And then we've got to convince people to come and help us.'

'Well, you're convincing me I've got to get out of here. So, why don't we just send off the photographs we've got? Why are they not good enough?'

'Because, if I've seen them, they may be dubious, and they're for sale, but they're not that worried about them being seen. They're not that worried that somebody's going to come for them. Just say I sent them off. Say I sent a photograph. He can't be that worried about those. And Clarissa hasn't got the world racing here after them.'

'Maybe she doesn't understand the situation. Maybe she doesn't understand that we're in trouble,' said Jane.

'If that property were so hot that people wanted it, Clarissa would be here. She would fight hand, tooth and nail to come here and solve it. She'd be yelling at Interpol or whoever else.'

'You think he's got other things?'

'If he's got these here, and he's bringing people here to buy them, maybe this is where he stores them. Maybe this is his hideaway. But it's done with an openness to say, this is what I'm making, making chemicals that people don't want to make themselves. It's an excellent reason for him to be where he is. It looks a little dirty, a bit nefarious, but it's actually legal. And people will look at it and say, "Oh yes, that's what's happening. But instead, he's doing something much worse.'

'Isn't that a bit of a jump?' said Jane.

'Of course it's a jump. It's a theory. At the moment, we've got our backs against the wall. All I've got is theory. Yes? All I've got is theory to go on. I'm postulating; I'm putting forward an idea to get us out of here. Because if it isn't true, and we are in some backwater and he's not doing anything particularly bad, we are in trouble,' said Seoras, fighting not to raise his voice.

The pig beside them grunted. 'So, what do we do?' asked Jane. 'Where do we go? Do we go to the medical centre?'

'Yes, we do,' said Seoras. 'That's where we go. We try to find out who the man is. Get some links. Work out the angle of what's happening. And then work out what we do next.'

Jane turned over and pulled Seoras tight. 'Sorry I got us in here,' she said. 'You didn't want to come all this way. You wanted a normal, basic holiday. Just to—' He put his hand up to her lips, stopping her speaking.

'You didn't cause this. Somebody shot someone dead. It happens.'

'It doesn't happen that often,' said Jane.

'In my world, in my life, it happens.'

'You're in a different world now. You're—'

'We are where we are, is what I'm saying. Not your fault. It's nobody's fault. It's just what is. So, we get on with it. We get out. There're times you have to trust yourself. Trust your abilities. Trust your skills. I need to trust you. Come on,' he said.

Seoras sat up inside the stye and then carefully worked his way out towards where a panel slid back. The sun was bright, causing him to squint. Looking around, he couldn't see anyone. Taking Jane's hand, he helped her out, and he closed the pigpen back up. He ran to the side of the house. There was a tap, and he turned it on, bending over and drinking from it, then showing Jane should to.

'We don't know if it's clean.'

'It's a tap; it'll be as clean as you get here, and we need fluid if we're going to be out in the sun.'

He was thankful he still had his fedora with him, popping it on his head. He looked at Jane's hair. It would be a decent shield from the sun.

'Maybe, you might tie something around your head or we can get you a hat,' he said.

'Where's the medical centre?' asked Jane. 'How far from here? Do you remember?'

'We're a little away from it. If we stick close to the roads, we'll be able to find it, though.'

'It'll be on the track back up towards the main compound.'

'We don't want to walk too close to the road,' Seoras said. 'We don't want to be too close to the shore either, in case they've got boats looking. Striking across country is the answer.'

He heard a vehicle and instinctively crouched down, glancing around the corner of the building. Out on the road, a Jeep rolled past with several guards scanning this way and that.

'Yes, we go cross-country,' he said. 'We need to find as much cover as we can in the scrubland and stay close to it.'

He looked at Jane. She gave him a faint smile.

'We got the phone, hats, cover. Have we got a bottle anywhere?' he asked. Jane looked back over toward the pigpen. There was a bottle stuck on one side, where water would drip into the pigs' trough. Seoras ran over, picked it up and brought it back to the tap, rinsing it out. He then filled it. There was no lid, but he would carry it with him.

'Water, because it will be hot,' he said. 'When we're in the medical centre, we can see where we can find food. Our job is to stay alive, find out information, and find someone who'll come to rescue us. If that fails, well then, we grab a boat and we go. You ready?'

Jane stepped forward, pulled him down to her and kissed him. 'Whatever happens,' she said, 'I don't regret it. I don't regret being with you.'

'Don't,' he said. 'Don't be emotional; step back from it. You need to go into this with a professional mindset.'

'Seoras, it's not what I did. I handed out tickets to people who parked their cars in the wrong place. This is your world.'

'Oh no,' said Seoras. 'Right now, this is our world, and you need to be detached. You need to not be emotional.'

'I am what I am,' she said.

He smiled. 'This is our world. You're going to have to embrace it.'

Chapter 21

'I'm famished,' said Jane, as Seoras handed over the bottle containing the last of their water.

'Drink it. It's hot out here. Drink it.'

'You haven't had much. You have it too,' she said.

'There's a small village up ahead. The medical centre's got to be close to that.'

'I haven't got any energy,' said Jane. 'We're out half the night. I can't.'

Seoras's stomach growled heavily.

'We need to eat,' said Jane.

'We do. Maybe they'll be some fruit off the trees or some—'

'Seoras, shut up,' said Jane. 'You said we had to embrace it, yes? Embrace where we are. We're going to that house over there, and we're going to nick some food.' Seoras raised his eyebrow. 'Seoras, it isn't a choice. We need to eat. We're hungry. I don't go around stealing food back in the UK. Don't go down to my local supermarket and just whiz the stuff off the shelf and drive off without paying. I am up against it here. So are you. No, we need to eat. We're going into that house. We're going to find what's there, and we're going to eat it. And if somebody comes in on us, we will tie them up, gag them.'

'You make that bit sound so easy,' said Seoras. 'We're going to tie them up. We're going to—'

'You're a policeman, trained how to fight. You must know how to fight dirty,' said Jane.'

'I'm afraid Clarissa was the expert on that.'

'You'll know how to do it. If you have to, you'll do it.'

Seoras nodded. He was so far out of his comfort zone, he was struggling. But Jane was right. He had told her to be practical, that she had to embrace where they were at. So, he needed to as well. He needed to get food.

Carefully, watching the road to make sure no cars were coming, he ran across it, Jane following him up the side of the house. He listened to hear if anyone was in but there was no noise. He opened the screen door at the side and stepped in to a basic-looking kitchen. There was fruit sitting in a bowl, and he walked over and grabbed it, pulling out his shirt and tumbling the fruit into it.

Behind him, Jane came in, opened up the refrigerator, and started pulling some items out. She then closed the door and whispered to him,

'Come on, we need to go.'

They quickly stepped back outside. As they did so, they heard a car and raced around the back of the house. The car stopped at the house, and someone could be heard getting out of the car and walking down the side of the house.

A door opened, and Seoras pointed along the back of the house. Together, the two of them ran, skipping a small fence into the dusty expanse that doubled as a garden for the house behind. Macleod went tight up against a wall, indicating Jane do the same.

'Eat,' he said. 'Eat now. No point carrying it.' He tore into some fruit. The juice was pouring down from his mouth, and his shirt got dripped in some sort of pink-staining juice from whatever fruit he was eating. Jane handed over what looked like a breast of chicken, and he ripped his teeth into it. In the space of five minutes, they woofed down all of the food, leaving behind all the skins.

'Shall we tidy it up?' asked Jane.

'Bird or something will come for it. Let's go,' he said. 'We need to keep moving.'

Seoras crept around the rear of the house, back across the road, and followed some trees up the far side. It was another twenty minutes before they spied the medical centre. It looked reasonably busy, and Seoras wondered how to get in.

There was a Jeep outside, a Land Rover too, and a couple of other vehicles. Jane told Seoras to wait, and she peered up and down the road, much in the fashion that he had, before running across and opening the side door of one vehicle. She came back across the road, carrying a couple of white overcoats.

'We go in as doctors, or go in as orderly staff,' she said. 'It might get us there.'

Together, they put on the coats, strolled across the road, and went up to the front door. Seoras whispered over his shoulder.

'Whatever you do, act like we are what we are. Don't flinch, don't say anything else.'

Seoras walked in, Jane following, and he turned and spoke to her about a patient. Random details came from his mouth, and he gave a nod to the woman who was sitting behind the desk.

She didn't look up from her magazine, and he turned down a corridor, past the patient waiting area.

'Which way?'

'This way,' said Jane. 'They brought me this way.'

She turned down through a wing of the building and onto a corridor, which had different private rooms.

'At the bottom,' she said. 'There was a station at the bottom, a doctor's room of some sort.'

Jane walked down and opened the door just as other doors were being opened in the corridor. Glancing inside, she saw no one and entered. Seoras followed her, closing the door behind him.

'Get to work,' he said, and he held the door closed tight. He looked to see if he could lock it and then saw a small bolt that could be put across. He did so.

'What if somebody comes?' she asked.

'We'll think of something, okay?'

Jane stared at the computer in front of her. As she moved the mouse, a password screen came up.

'It's no good, Seoras. They've got a network. I need to know how to get onto the network.'

'Lock the door when I go out,' said Seoras, unbolting the door. He stepped outside, closing the door behind him, and looked up and down the corridor. Pulling his white coat tight, he marched along, his fedora down over the top of his head. He kept his head bowed as he walked past people, up and down several corridors before he saw it.

It was the staff room. Seoras opened the door and stepped inside. A number of people were relaxing, most engaged in their phones or a book. Seoras walked over to the sideboard, picked up a mug and poured a coffee. He drank it, looking up at a notice board. There was various information, thankfully in English, about rotations of staff, which he ignored. Others told about procedures and something about hand washing.

There was a schedule of when deliveries were being made.

Then he saw it. A small piece of paper in the bottom corner. It was the general staff login to the system for temporary staff. Looking briefly over his shoulder to make sure everyone was engaged in whatever they were doing on their break, he grabbed the piece of paper. Stuffing it in his pocket, he downed his coffee, looked for a sink, rinsed it out, set it to one side and left the room.

When he got back, he tapped on the door. 'Jane, it's me.' She opened it, closed the door behind her and Seoras handed over the login details. 'Try that,' he said. 'It's a generic login.'

Jane did so. 'I've got the internet,' she said. 'Let's have a look then, see what we can get.'

'Can you search his face? We used to always search faces in the Force. It was very good.'

'But you have a database for that in the police. I don't think Ross would have been searching Google.'

'But can we?'

'The only face we've got,' said Jane, 'is on the phone now. I can probably get off the phone and onto the system here, but it's a dead man. It's a man with his head half blown off.'

'Well, put that up,' said Seoras.

'I can't put a dead man's face up on Google. It'll go crazy. You know, they scan photos like that. It'll draw attention.'

'What do we do then?' asked Seoras.

'Hang on,' said Jane. She logged in to an AI site she had used before.

'What have you got this for?'

'I was messing about. You can change people's pictures and stuff. I was looking to do greetings cards and things. Just some fun stuff while I was at home.'

Seoras eyed the screen suspiciously.

'But this is my private account,' continued Jane. 'It doesn't show anybody else. So I can upload the image, mess about and then delete it. And nobody knows what's there. It's only if I share it afterwards out to the world that they see it. I need to upload the photograph.'

She went onto the phone's gallery and then stopped as the photograph came up on the screen. Jane put her hand to her mouth and turned away.

'Breathe,' said Seoras. 'Breathe. Force it back down. Breathe. Relax. Breathe.'

Seoras put his hands on her shoulders, and then he opened the door, disappearing outside. He grabbed a bedpan that was sitting on a trolley in the corridor and came back in. He put it in front of Jane as she let go, vomiting into the bedpan.

With the door locked behind him, the stink was suffocating. But he turned her back to the screen. 'Upload it. Do what you're going to do,' he said. 'You have to do this.'

Jane sat, shaking, as she uploaded the picture. And from there, she asked the AI to adjust it. A man's face came up with no hole in the head. No hair missing. No dead eyes. Seoras was amazed. It was so close. He hadn't known the man when he was alive, so this was certainly a guess of sorts, but it looked good. Jane closed the screen down quickly after having obtained her new image. She now put the new image into an image search on Google. She then tried other search engines. Eventually, there was a hit.

It was close. It was the man's face, but it was rather strange. She went through the link, and it was to a newspaper, but it was Arabic. She looked at the pictures. There was a jewel in one picture. There was a Saudi prince. And then there was the man, but he had a placard below his face.

'He's a criminal,' said Seoras. 'I can't read that, but he's a criminal.'

'He is, isn't he?' said Jane. 'Maybe it's the jewel. Maybe he's stolen from that prince. Do you think?' Seoras stood looking. 'Hang on a minute,' said Jane.

She scrolled up until there was a button to translate the page. She clicked on it and waited. The English that came back was far from perfect, but in the pidgin English that was there, the man was a wanted criminal. He had stolen the jewel belonging to a Saudi prince.

'That's who we need,' said Seoras. 'That's who we need to contact.'

'Well, I could try to contact him.'

'But with what?' said Seoras. 'All we're going to do is show him the dead man's body. His dead face. We want him to come to help us. We need to find that jewel. He'll have brought it here. That's what it will be about. We know that Wainwright sells. We know Wainwright was bringing people to deal with. Well, maybe that jewel's in the house or in the chemical plant compound. Probably the compound, because, well, he won't want it to be in the house, will he? The house held all the guests. You've got to put a jewel like that somewhere safe. He wouldn't have shown us something like that.'

'It's a bit of a long shot, isn't it?' said Jane.

'It's the only shot we've got. If we can get an image of that jewel, the prince will come for it. I mean, these are Saudi princes, aren't they? They've got money; they've got people.'

'Have you met many?' asked Jane.

'I've never met any.'

'So, you're kind of hoping?'

'I'm working with what I've got. But even if it isn't in there, we can take something else. If we can take something away, we can bargain with, that will help. We need to have something.'

There was a noise outside.

'Close it down, everything. Get everything off,' said Seoras.

He opened the door, stepped outside, and went back to the trolley, which was sitting in the middle of the corridor. He reached down and grabbed a couple of face masks and hairnets. Back inside the room, he closed the door again.

'It's all shut down,' said Jane.

Seoras handed over one of the face masks and a hairnet before putting a mask on along with the hairnet. He put his fedora hat inside his jacket, making his stomach look much bigger than it was.

'Let's go,' he said. 'We need to get out of here.'

They turned and walked out along a corridor. As they strode along, they could hear noises. There were arguments going on as they made for the front door. Seoras stopped. Some of the guards had come into the medical centre. They were harassing the staff, asking if they'd seen anyone.

Seoras turned on his heel, but as he did so, he saw a guard coming down the other way. He looked to the left. X-ray. He turned, opened the door and marched in, Jane following. He turned down another corridor and then saw an emergency exit. Seoras took his jacket off, threw the mask and the hairnet down, plonked his fedora on his head, pushed open the emergency exit and stepped outside. Jane copied him but threw the coats inside a nearby toilet. As soon as he closed the emergency door behind him, Seoras ran as hard as he could over to a nearby house. There he stopped, hiding behind a wall as Jane caught up.

'They might know somebody's been in there, with those coats left around,' said Jane.

'Maybe, but we'll get on the move. Head towards the compound. It's the last place they'll think we'll go. And when we get there, we'll work out how to get inside.'

'How do we get inside?' asked Jane.

Seoras stared at her. 'I'm making it up as I go along at the moment. I told you; you just have to embrace it.'

She took his hand. It was shaking. Cool, calm DCI Macleod was shaking. She realised just how much trouble they were in.

Chapter 22

Night had fallen, but Seoras was happy that darkness was their friend. They were closer to the compound now, and he had slowed down. He had stopped trekking along, and took every movement at a slow pace. Jane was getting in the way of it as well, always watching, always looking to see if anyone was about.

He reckoned that a lot of the guards were out searching the rest of the island. They must have assumed Jane and he would try to get away. Get to boats or planes. Certainly, not come back towards the compound. Seoras knew well that everything he was doing at the moment was instinct. A hunch, a guess. The diamond would be in the compound, not in the house.

The compound would have the real strong rooms. After all, that's what you did when you had things. You hid them in places that people didn't think they would be. A room in a house would be the perfect place to hold a jewel. You could come in every morning to look at it, but in a chemical compound, in a place where they made nasty chemicals, the idea would seem strange. It's not where you would naturally see it, but it was perfect if you had the mind for these sorts of things.

You had lots of reasons for keeping people out. Good reasons. You were making nasty stuff so they couldn't barge or force their way in. They'd be careful about what they did because of what was around them. If Wainwright was going to store a hidden jewel, Seoras reckoned he wouldn't put it in a fancy secure room in his large house, making it an obvious target. He would store it in plain sight. The man, if his hunch was correct, had created an entire island resort and had taken on an industry that was dubious and caused many problems, just as cover.

Seoras felt the dryness of his throat. They'd eaten earlier that day—or rather, thrown food into themselves—but he had had nothing since. His stomach was complaining again. Jane was maybe only about ten feet behind, and Seoras waved her up as they got within view of the compound. He was lying on his front now, at the top of a small rise, and Jane lay down beside him.

'So how do we get in?' she said.

'There are guards patrolling the front, a high fence, I don't think you and I are going to jump over that.'

'Well certainly not you,' said Jane, causing Seoras to look at her. 'Do we walk up to the guards and say, "Let us in."'

'One of us might have to cause a diversion, while the other one gets inside,' suggested Seoras.

'I don't like that thought,' she said, 'splitting up.'

'I don't like it either; quite a risk too; one of us could end up being captured, being taken inside, if we run a diversion.'

'Well then, let's not. Let's work out how we get in together. There must be quieter ways to do it, places we could climb round and enter through.'

'Jane,' said Seoras, 'the places you climb round, over fences, and drop into are usually done by people with some degree of gymnastic ability. I don't mean to be rude, love, but that's not us.'

Jane went to quip back, but he was right. Jane looked around her, and then she thought she heard something. 'Seoras,' she said quietly, 'do you hear feet?'

He did, from behind. Seoras couldn't stand up, for fear someone saw him. But behind him , they'd be looking up to him. It was the front view he was protected from, the side a little, but behind he had no protection.

'Maybe crawl forward,' he said. 'Stay on your belly.' He went to move, and then he heard the sound that caused him to shake.

'Don't move,' said a voice. Feet walked up behind him, and then he felt the point of a gun in the back of his neck. 'Don't move, don't say a word. You're going to rise slowly to your feet when I tell you to. You're going to slowly—'

There was a loud thunk. The gun disappeared from the back of his neck. Beside Seoras lay a guard, sprawled out flat.

Seoras slowly looked over his shoulder, and there was the young woman, who had pulled them out of the boat.

'You want to be coming this way,' she whispered. 'Stay down low. You too,' she said to Jane. Quickly, the woman half crouched as she scampered along, Seoras and Jane following her.

The woman said nothing more but showed with her hands when they should follow her, and eventually clambered down a rock face and into a small cove area. It was steep, not an easy descent, but Seoras and Jane made it, and arriving at the bottom, they were taken inside a small cave. There, sitting around a small portable heater, was the young man who had saved their life.

'Good, she got you,' he said as they entered. 'I was worried. We'd had reports of your moving up the west side of the island. I didn't know if you'd get this far. Bit of an amateurish place to look from, though. You need to remember to cover all sides, DCI Macleod.'

Seoras raised his eyebrows, whereas Jane audibly gasped. 'I know who you are,' said the man. 'Why are you sneaking about in the middle of the night, though?'

'I'd have thought you might have known that,' said Seoras, 'if you know my name.'

'I don't know all the details,' said the man. 'Lara here was good enough to go pick you up. I was going to do it myself but she's good.'

'I'm well aware of that,' said Seoras. 'You've saved our lives already. You've been close by often. It's one of the best covers I've seen. But I thought you were somebody else. Just too often, too regularly, appearing when we needed help or at strange times.

'And you ran into the water starkers. Are you a couple?' asked Jane.

'They're running excellent cover,' said Seoras. 'One of the best ways is to make people a little embarrassed, be outgoing. After all, you wouldn't have a couple of agents or spies running around in the buff, would you? People don't like that, drawing attention to themselves. But you drew it the right way. You drew it in a way that says we can't be anything but a young, excitable couple.'

'Very good, DCI Macleod. I'd heard you had a brain on you. I'm not disappointed. Why are you going into the compound? What could possibly make you go in there?'

'Do you want to tell me who you are first?' asked Seoras.

'No,' said the man. 'But I've helped you, and that should be enough for you. We helped you again. You owe us a bit of an explanation. But call me Fred if it helps.'

Seoras looked from the man to the woman. 'Well, Jane, on one of our first days here, saw a man being shot at the rear of the chemical compound, in the head. She then tried to return to me but passed out. We weren't sure if she'd hallucinated or not, but suddenly the governor took an interest in us. I've been accosted by a strange woman, and on my travels around, I've also found a shallow grave. In the middle of last night, I dug that grave up, unzipped a very modern body bag, and took a photograph of the face of a man.

'We got into the medical centre and adjusted the photograph of the face so we could search it up on the World Wide Web. His picture turned up in an Arabic newspaper. The rough translation seemed to say he was a thief and had taken a priceless gem from a Saudi prince. Prince Assam, I think it said. I believe the jewel could be inside the compound.

'It's not in the house, or at least not on show in the house because I've been in there. But the compound would be a great place to hide it. I think the governor steals artworks and holds them here and sells them on. I'm doing this because there's no other way for me to get off this island, without being taken hold of by the governor again. They want us dead. Especially now, for they know Jane has seen something, and I've also seen the body. So, they won't let us walk out of here. Keeping silent was not an option.'

'Very good, DCI Macleod.'

'Just Seoras will do.'

'So, the two of you were going to break in there. How?' asked

Lara.

'I don't know,' Seoras said to them both. 'That's what we were trying to work out. And in our defence, we've kept ourselves out of trouble for quite a while. They haven't found us yet. Or at least they hadn't until Laura here had to intervene. So you've been watching us closely. And you live in open sight. You must be spies of some sort. Who do you work for?'

'A good spy would never tell you that. And I'm a good one,' said Fred. 'However, I am intrigued by what you're saying. I'll get you inside the facility. You've been pursued, and so getting inside the facility will be difficult because they have enough guards on. However, I will cause a diversion. I will get you inside the compound, and I will create a further diversion, and you can search. When you get out with the jewel, we will meet up again, and then we'll talk more, and I'll get you the hell out of here.'

'That sounds like a plan,' said Seoras.

'Stay here,' said the man. 'We'll be back.' He said something to Lara, and the two of them disappeared outside the cave they were in. Jane cuddled up to Seoras.

'Is this the help we needed? Are these the people we wanted?'

'I don't know. The jewel seems to be a real thing. After all, they're going to get us inside. And if we do, we'll look. However, they may be getting us inside to create a diversion for them. They're definitely on the opposite side of Wainwright, but they also wanted to keep us alive. That gives me a lot of hope and a lot of trust in them. However, it's not a black and white science. It's hard to read people. It's hard to read intentions, especially when you haven't got a clue what's going on. So we'll go along with it, but we'll keep our eyes open.'

Jane cuddled into Seoras. It was about an hour later when

the couple returned.

'It's time to go,' Fred said. 'Hope you're warm enough. There are a couple of energy bars in there you can eat before we go, but then we do it.' He pointed to the bag Lara had thrown on the floor. 'Grab some water and drink it. I assume you've been struggling for food on the move.'

'They don't train us as detectives for survival. They train us how to arrest people. So I'm afraid I'm a little out of my zone just now. And Jane's a traffic warden. Actually, she might be better trained for this.' Jane grinned at Seoras' attempt to lighten the mood.

'Yes indeed,' said the man. 'Eat up, drink up, then we go.'

Having fully satisfied themselves with a couple of bars and some water to drink, they reached the top of the climb above the cave. Seoras and Jane were led along until they came to the road where there was a Jeep.

The rear of it had a covering tarpaulin, allowing anything in the back of it to be stored, safe from the rain. And the couple indicated that Seoras and Jane should get in there. As the Jeep then bumped along, Seoras felt himself jostled. Jane held her hand in his.

'It's not the most comfortable,' she hissed.

'Keep it silent,' Seoras said. 'We'll be going through the check before the compound. We don't want to give the game away with random noises.'

Jane gripped his hand, and the Jeep continued through the night until eventually it stopped. There were some words spoken, and then the Jeep rumbled on. It turned a few corners here and there before stopping. After a moment, there was a voice whispering through the canvas above them.

'Two minutes, Seoras,' said a voice. 'Then get yourself out.

You're inside the main compound. There'll be a door on your far side. Enter that and you're inside. After that, it's up to you. I know no more than you do about the interior. We will be elsewhere to create a diversion. We've arrived, however, in a guard's Jeep. No one will look twice at this, so make sure you leave it that way. Get inside and stay quiet.

'The part of the complex we're in at the moment seems to be quiet. Automated, a few people about. I thought that might be the area he would store a secret room in. Best chance of it being seen by the fewest people. Good luck, Detective Chief Inspector. And you too, his good lady.'

And then there was nothing. Seoras held Jane's hand, squeezing it tightly. He could feel her shaking, and no wonder for his heart was pounding. Seoras was just controlling his body a lot better. Starting a count, he reached one hundred and twenty before pushing up and pulling the canvas back off himself. He clambered out of the Jeep, helped Jane down, and then pulled the canvas back over.

Quickly, they made for the door the man had indicated. There were plenty of warning signs around it. Chemicals, air defenders required, hard hats. It had all the signs of a normal working area, a factory of sorts.

As soon as they got inside the door, Jane said to him, 'So what are we looking for?'

Seoras turned to her. 'A place where you store an incredibly valuable jewel amid a fully functioning chemical plant.'

'What does that place look like?' asked Jane.

'I have no idea,' said Seoras. 'Keep your eyes open.'

Chapter 23

Scoras looked up and down the corridor he was in. There were metal grilles on the floor, and as he walked, they rang out. He tried to walk quietly, Jane shushing him from behind.

'Where do we go?' she asked.

'I don't know. We need to find it. It'll be in something, some sort of room. Some sort of—'

'Should we split up?'

'If we split up, we'll never find each other again. Come on.'

He took her hand and walked in one direction. The sides of the walls had pipes running along them, with coloured tape on the pipe. He could hear the occasional clanking and what sounded like pumps.

The floor turned into a gangway and went off in two directions—one straight ahead and one hard to the right. On either side of the right turn, large vats made of what he thought was stainless steel could be heard bubbling. He walked between them, but there was nothing.

Scoras spun around seeking inspiration. On the sides were coloured panels. Pump numbers indicated. Levels. Again, he had no idea what he was looking at.

'He's not going to put it in the middle of all this stuff, is he?' asked Jane.

'Why?' asked Seoras.

'If you're going to take it, and if it's that good, you're going to want to look at it. You're going to have to have somewhere that you step inside and you look at it. It's going to be presented. Otherwise, what's the point of having it?'

'The money,' said Seoras. 'He wants the money when he sells it on. He's just got to keep it hidden. Somewhere to hang onto it. He's got to—'

'It won't be here. Come on, let's look further,' she said. And this time, she dragged him. Jane went to turn a corner on the gangway and suddenly stopped pulling backwards. 'Somebody's there,' she said. 'There's somebody there.'

'Well, let's not go that way,' said Seoras. He turned and went in the opposite direction, and then walked around a corner, straight into an employee. The man looked him up and down.

'What are you doing here?' he said in an American accent.

'I appear to be a bit lost,' said Seoras, turning to explain that Jane was with him. Jane wasn't there. He could hear footsteps on the grille, but there had been another person further back. And then he saw, from behind the man, a figure approaching. They were holding a large spanner, the sort you would use on a giant nut.

His eyes widened, and the man talking to him suddenly panicked, wondering what Seoras was looking at. He turned just as the large spanner caught him on the top of the hard hat, knocking him down to the floor. There was a loud clang, the spanner falling, and Jane looking half-shocked at what she'd done. Seoras could hear footsteps coming along the metal gangways now.

He grabbed her hand, hurdled the man who had collapsed on the ground, and ran off in that direction. He cut back, down towards the door they'd come in originally, and ran past it, further into the complex.

As he ran along, he realised that there weren't that many people. The corridor suddenly opened out. Seoras could see a room at the top of some metal stairs, one from which you could look down on the entire operation in this part of the facility. Maybe it was the control room.

There wasn't anybody in it as far as he could make out. Seoras saw the staircase that wound round squarely, and he tore off in that direction, Jane following. Round and round they went until they reached the door at the top, which said control room. Seoras opened it and stepped inside, and a man turned, looking shocked.

Seoras drove himself at him, caught the man in the midriff, who again looked shocked, as he hit the back wall. Seoras caught his own head on the wall, tumbling off to one side. The man looked groggy, and as Seoras looked up from the floor, unable to keep his own feet, he saw Jane grab a chair. She threw it into the man. The man stumbled back again, hit his head on the wall, and crumpled.

Jane turned and closed the door of the control room. She crept forward to the large window and looked out. 'I'm not seeing anyone out there. I'm not seeing . . .'

And then she stopped as she looked round at Seoras. He was lying on the floor, feeling a bit knocked about.

'What?' he said. 'I hit him with what I had.'

'No, your hat.'

'What about my hat?' His hat had come off his head and was now sitting in front of a door. The door had no label on it.

'What about in there?' she said.

Seoras groggily got to his feet and pulled open the door. 'It's just lots and lots of cabinets,' he said.

'Well, pull a few of them open.'

He did so, and there before him was an arrangement of stones. It looked like a display from a Museum of Natural History—different samples of rocks.

'They're all listed,' said Seoras.' He pulled out some drawers with bits of rock and notelets. 'This is identification for the process. This must be—' And then he stopped.

A drawer close to the bottom was pulled open and Seoras could see what looked like diamonds. Or at least precious stones. There were labels beside some of them. One did indeed say diamond. Others said ruby and sapphire, and other names that he wasn't so familiar with.

'Jane, get in here a minute,' he said. 'Look, do you think those are stolen ones?'

'You think those are—' started Jane, and Seoras shook his head.

'How do I know? I was asking you. I don't know what's real. Haven't a clue if these are samples or what.'

And then Jane's face lit up. 'Hide it. Hide it somewhere where you can see it,' she said. 'Look! Look in the corner.'

There was a cabinet, containing a light box of some sort. 'What's that?' asked Seoras.

Jane reached down and picked up a purported ruby, took it over to the light box, opened the device's door, placed the ruby in the middle, and then flipped the switch. The ruby lit up, with light beaming through it. She beamed at Seoras.

'It's here. It'll be here. He can come, he can look at the stone, but it looks like nothing. It looks just like a sample, just like

201

these other rocks, just like—'

Seoras turned back. 'Well, where is it?' he asked. 'Where is it, then?' He picked up one stone after another until Jane slapped his hand.

'Stop it,' she said. 'Let me look.' And then she pointed. 'That's the one in the picture,' she said. Jane took the stone she had indicated, ran over to the light box, put it inside and switched it on.

'Well,' Seoras asked, 'is that definitely the one?'

Jane stood and looked at him. 'I don't know why I did that,' she said. 'I have no idea. You have as much idea about what I'm looking at as I do. But it looks like the right shape. Yep, that looks like the one.'

'What's the name on it?'

'Massa,' she said. 'It says Massa. What's Massa? Is Massa a stone?'

Seoras looked at some of the other names. He had no idea they were stones. 'Hang on,' he said. 'The prince who it was stolen from was called Assam. Massa is Assam backwards.'

Jane grabbed the jewel from the light box. 'We need to get out of here,' she said.

'We do,' Seoras said. 'Come on, let's go quickly.' They stepped back into the control room and tore down the descending square stairs until they reached the gangway. They could hear noises, people running here and there.

'I'm not sure where to go.'

'If we head back, we could get into the Jeep and we could bust out,' urged Jane excitedly.

'No,' said Seoras. 'We can't drive out. They'd see us. You can't drive through a fence or that with that Jeep either. We need to get out another way. We need to—'

'If we got to the rear where I saw him shot,' said Jane, 'if we got there, there are the rocks. You can descend to the sea. Get out that way.'

'And do what? Clamber round?'

'Yes,' said Jane. 'We could clamber round. Get up onto the cliff top. We know the route; we saw it from the sea. We know the way.'

'And then we'd have to run for cover again.'

'Or find that cove. Find that cove and find that couple.'

'I have a feeling they may find us,' said Seoras. 'But how do we get out? We need a map of some sort.'

Jane slapped him on the side. 'The control room. The control room will have a map, won't it? A map of the entire facility. That's how we get out. Seoras, back up the steps.'

'I've got to go all the way back up? My knees are shot.'

'Well, you can stand here while I go up and have a look,' she said. 'But you're going to stick out.'

The two turned and tore their way back up. As they got back inside the control room, the man they'd knocked over previously was just getting up on his feet. Seoras ran over and dived at him with his shoulder, knocking the man back again into the wall. He slumped down, moaning.

Meanwhile, Jane was getting giddy with excitement.

'I've got it,' she said. 'I've got it. We just simply—'

Seoras put his hand up. 'He's not out. He's not out cold. Just go. I'll follow.'

Jane raced out of the control room. She was puffing now, out of breath, but not nearly so much as Seoras was. He focused on his feet, scrambling down the descending staircase, and then they were down again.

'This way,' she said, and legged it along metal gangways. She cut left and right, and then she cut right again. And then they were in a corridor. They passed by what looked like a toilet as they heard voices up ahead. Jane pushed open the door. It had the sign of a woman on it, and she hauled Seoras inside.

There were toilets there, and she pulled him inside one of the cubicles, placing her feet on the ground. He lifted his up, stepping onto the toilet and crouching down behind her. The feet outside ran past the door, and Jane stood up, opening the cubicle door, hauling Seoras after her. She quickly opened the toilets' door, looked left and right, and continued her progress.

There were two more doors she went through, holding the map up in front of her, and then suddenly they were outside in the dark. As they ran forward, lights came on from all directions. Seoras froze, waiting to hear guns being cocked, waiting to be told to put his hands up.

But there was silence.

'Automatic lights,' said Jane. 'This is it. This is where it happened. They took him out here. Look over there.'

Jane kept running, and Seoras, puffing hard, ran after her. He saw her at a gate. She pushed it open. An alarm sounded, but Jane was already through the gate, running down rocks and then approaching the sea. But she slipped, and Seoras watched as she went right over the edge of what rocks he could see.

He scrambled down as quickly as he could. Looking down into the sea, he saw waves crashing about. Jane was being flung here and there. He had to go. He had to try to save her.

He was not, like his former partner, Hope McGrath, was. She was a competent swimmer. She could dive, and he'd seen her several times in action, saving people in the water. Instead, Seoras simply jumped, his feet out in front of him, and crashed down into the waves below. He was thrown this way and that, gasping, but he was pulled out to sea, and soon he was out of the main swirl, floating. He remembered what they said. Float to live. Putting his arms out, he leaned back, trying to catch his breath, and then he heard a voice.

'Seoras! Seoras!' It was Jane. And then there was a spotlight on him.

Seoras heard the engine of an approaching boat followed by more shouts.

'Seoras!'

He looked over. Jane was on the deck of a yacht. A motorised yacht. A yacht he recognised. Eamon was at the helm. Jane was leaning over the edge now, soaking wet, but she had a large pole with a hook on it.

Seoras grabbed it. He clambered on board, and the yacht turned away, heading out to sea. But it hadn't got far when it idled. Seoras was still on the lower deck, breathing heavily. Jane had her arm around him.

'You okay?' she asked desperately. 'Are you all right?'

'Well, I hope you're all right,' said a voice. 'What the blazes were you doing jumping into the sea like that?'

Seoras looked up and saw Eamon pointing a gun at him. 'What do you mean, what were we doing? Seoras asked. 'Why are you here?'

'Do you have it?' asked Eamon. He walked closer, the gun pointing directly at Seoras.

'I wondered what you were,' said Seoras. 'I still don't know what you are.'

'Do you have it? I won't ask again.'

Jane reached into her pocket and took out the gem. 'I have it.'

Seoras took it off Jane. 'This. This is what you want. Why

do you want it?'

'I'll take it, if you please.'

'Why? What could you want with it? Have you really been here three years? Have you really been here all this time?'

'Give it to me,' said Eamon. 'Don't mess about. I don't want to harm you, but I will do. If I need to.' Seoras pushed Jane behind him and then stepped forward slowly, the jewel in his hand. Eamon slowly crept towards him, then reached out with one hand, taking the gem and holding it up in front of him. He stared at it. Seoras took the moment and swiped a hand, knocking the gun to the floor.

He then crashed into Eamon, who dropped, and the jewel slid across the deck. Jane cried out as Eamon grappled with Seoras on the deck. Neither of the men were in the throes of youth, but Eamon was stronger, grabbing Seoras by the neck. His hand came up over Seoras' face, but Seoras was a man who had walked the streets of Glasgow, a man who had taken on the best of them.

And he bit him hard in the hand, and then he bit him in the arm, and then he swung an elbow into his face. He heard Jane run off, and then the engine of the boat started. Eamon rolled away to one side, and then he shouted.

'What are you doing? Eejit! Don't!'

Seoras had just about got back to his feet when the boat, going full astern, rammed into the rocks. It threw everyone to one side. The gun slid past Seoras, and he grabbed it and threw it off into the sea. Jane came running towards Seoras, who was groggily getting onto his feet. As she did so, she held up the jewel.

'Go, we need to go!'

Eamon got up on his feet, but the boat lurched again, and

he stumbled across, smacking his head on a fixture. Jane and Seoras slid, but they caught the rope around the edge of the yacht before scrambling off onto rocks at the stern of the vessel. Heading off into the night, Seoras looked back briefly.

Eamon was lying on the deck. *Where would they go? The boat would have been a good getaway. There was comms on that boat too.* Heading into the night, Seoras wondered what he would do next. Jane looked over his shoulder. 'What now?'

'We run,' he said. 'We run!' It was all he had.

Chapter 24

The dawn was spectacular, but neither Seoras nor Jane had any time to watch. Inside, Seoras was feeling gutted. He should have seen Eamon coming. He knew the man had some allegiance somewhere, but he didn't know what it was. Apparently, he'd been looking for the jewel, but how did he know about the jewel? *Where had that come from? How did he know it had been in the compound and how did he know that they would have it?*

Seoras was a little confused. There were other things happening here that he didn't understand. *The couple who had helped them get into the compound, the couple who had helped them locate the jewel and confirmed its existence, at least the idea of it—what were they doing here? Who were they working for? Who were they a secret agent for? Surely not British.*

He had connections within the secret service, and they would have helped him more than that. In fact, they would have taken him out of the issue. They didn't work with amateurs such as him strolling about. The one time he'd gone to Italy to help a colleague, he had to be rescued by Kirsten; she had informed him how he didn't behave like a spy and was basically rubbish at it. And besides, he had Jane with him as well. And he was retired. There's no way they would let him do this.

Instead, were the couple with the Americans? But were they spies? He had assumed that, hadn't he? And they'd played the role. Had they just picked up and run with it? Were they agents for someone else. Eamon was clearly an agent for someone. But who? Had he been involved initially with the man who had died?

Had Eamon known him? Was he on his side? Was he there to retrieve the goods because payment hadn't been made? Is that what Wainwright had done? Who knew?

Frustrated, Seoras had no way of finding these things out. He didn't have a DCI's carte blanche where you wandered in and started interviewing people. He missed that, the arms and legs of his team around him, too. And he missed the authority he once carried. Seoras felt so vulnerable, so exposed, and such an inadequate shield for Jane.

'What do we do?' asked Jane.

'We need to get out of here. Out, out, completely.'

'But how? I mean, that bit's obvious.'

'I don't know. Hoped that Eamon might have been an option.'

'What's his deal?' asked Jane.

'Again, I don't know,' said Seoras. 'A lot of what I did in the past was working in the dark and it hasn't changed.'

'Sorry,' she said. 'I just keep looking to you. You're the expert. You're the—'

'I'm not an expert at this, trust me.'

'But you seemed so calm initially. So—'

'The exterior's an act. It always is. You're always wearing a face that says something to other people. Keep them in the dark about what you're really thinking. Like Eamon. He kept us in the dark.'

'Did he?' said Jane. 'Ultimately, he asked for the jewel. I mean, he might have just let us go after that. Might have taken the boat and dropped us off somewhere. He seemed quite kind.'

'He seemed quite kind? The man stuck a gun in our faces,' said Seoras.

'Only because he needed the jewel. Maybe he had to retrieve it for someone.'

'You think the best of people,' said Seoras.

'Well, I haven't had a lifetime of watching them kill each other.'

She turned away now from watching and sat looking at the interior of the room they occupied. 'What about that couple?'

'What about them?'

'Well, they're agents, aren't they? They must be working for somebody good.'

'Why?' asked Seoras.

'Well, they helped us. They helped us get in there. They ran a diversion to help us find this jewel.'

'And why did they do that? Were we running a diversion for them while they were off doing something else? Were they after the jewel, too? Are they part of Eamon's team? I mean, they turned up an awful lot. And Eamon was close by.'

'So, they just rescued us because they needed a diversion. But surely if we'd have got picked up and taken inside when we were outside the compound, that would have been a diversion.'

'A diversion to the people who would then torture us. Or at least question us. Maybe not to the guards outside.'

'But how did we run a diversion?'

'Because we were a couple of amateurs,' said Seoras.

'You're not an amateur.'

'I am. In this field, I am an amateur. Would you get that into your head?'

'Don't you shout at me,' said Jane. 'You might do that to those underlings you had, but I'm no underling. I'm half of this partnership. You talk to me properly.'

'Sorry,' he said. 'Just frustrated. They weren't underlings; they were friends.'

'That's not what I meant.' She gave a sigh and, on her knees, crawled over to the fridge in the room's corner, taking out some milk and drinking it.

'You're just taking that,' he said.

'We're on the run. I thought we had this discussion.'

'We're not on the run the same as before, though.'

'How? It's probably worse,' said Jane.

'Uh-oh,' said Seoras, 'there's somebody coming here, I hear Jeeps.'

'Oh, we've got to go out the back then, before they arrive.'

'They're coming up the driveway, let's go!' He turned, took her hand, and led her out the rear of the building. As they got there, he could see a small cloud in the distance, approaching the rear of the building. 'Looks like more of them,' he said.

'We'd better hide then. Let's get over towards the pigsty here.'

'I'm not going back in a pigsty,' he said. There was a chicken house, quite large, and numerous chickens around it. Seoras wondered if they would cluck. Surely any fuss from a chicken could be for anything. He took her hand and led her around the back of the chicken house. There was a lot of clucking going on, and he tried to soothe the hens, whispering quietly.

'Cluck, cluck,' he said.

Jane looked at him as if he were insane, and then glancing

211

around the chicken house, her face lit up. 'That's the couple. That's the couple in the Jeep. The one that's coming towards us now. It's the couple!'

The Jeep pulled up towards the rear of the house, and there were shouts coming from the front. Men shouting. The woman in the Jeep waved at Jane, screaming at her to get in.

She grabbed Seoras, and the two of them, as fast as they could, ran for the Jeep, jumping into the rear seats. The Jeep tore off, and behind them, several other Jeeps followed.

'Strap yourself in,' said the woman. They did so, and the Jeep careered off the road and across rough ground. Seoras held Jane's hand. He'd never been so afraid in a vehicle, and he'd been in the manic green sports car of DI Clarissa Urquhart.

She drove insanely. This man, in fairness, was driving away from danger, but he still seemed to have that insane lust for high and reckless speed. They cut down, past a boulder, then down another. Seoras flicked a look over his shoulder and saw one Jeep behind roll over. Their own Jeep careered the other way, off up on two wheels, then came down hard.

Seoras gripped the fedora on his head as he felt it about to lift off. He would not lose it. It was a gift after all. And then he thought of how ridiculous he was being. He grabbed the hat and pulled it down off his head, holding it tight with crossed hands to his stomach.

'We're going to make a run for the airport,' said the woman. 'It wasn't easy picking up your trail, but they were onto you as well. I don't know how easy it will be to shake these guys off, but we'll need to keep going. There are airplanes at the airport, private ones. I should be able to get several of us in one and get out of here. All we've got to do is land in somewhere like the Seychelles.

'It'll be a reasonable flight and they'll have nothing to come and take us out in the air. There's nothing that would prevent us from getting there once we can get airborne,' said Lara. She said this as the hair blew across her face, almost smiling. Seoras wasn't smiling, and neither was Jane. The idea of vomiting was closer to their minds. And they were going to have to run for it again.

The vehicle turned hard and headed up towards the compound in the island's north pursued now by two Jeeps. Possibly, they may have radioed ahead, and Seoras noted Fred was keeping them aimed towards the compound. The airfield was a little further over to the right of where they were.

He's going to let them call in, thought Seoras. *They're going to gather their troops up at the compound and then he's going to head for the airfield. Maybe I'm getting this agent thing.* Kirsten might have been proud of him, but in truth, he didn't have a clue. He was a backseat passenger on a hurtling vehicle desperately trying to escape armed men.

Seoras was right, however, and as they got closer towards the compound, the vehicle was suddenly spun right and across country towards the airfield. Airfield's back home in the UK would have protective barriers around them. Fences you couldn't get inside without going through multiple levels of security. When they'd stepped out on the island, the security hadn't been so prevalent, and the Jeep could drive straight onto the airfield. Albeit they'd have to go across very rough terrain.

There were several hangars towards the far end of the airfield, away from where they'd arrived and what could be seen as the public area. The Jeep continued, pursued by the two others, as a plane landed just across from them on the runway. Seoras thought this was madness, especially as the

Jeep then turned and went straight across the runway, not that far behind where the aircraft had been. They drove in through one of the open hangar doors. The Jeep was parked, and Fred ordered everyone out.

Seoras grabbed Jane and started running for an aircraft, but Lara shouted over, 'No, this way,' and she ran for the rear door of the hangar. Some bemused locals stood amazed as they disappeared out and ran around the back into another hangar. This one was closed up, but inside was a small fixed-wing aircraft with six seats inside.

Seoras followed Lara up to the cockpit, while Fred pulled away the stops holding the wheels in place. The foursome climbed inside, got strapped in, but just as Fred jumped in the front doors of the hangar opened and there were several Jeeps blocking their path. Slowly, the Jeeps approached, guns trained on them.

'Sorry, folks, we weren't quick enough,' mused Fred.

The guards surrounded the aircraft and, one by one, Seoras, Jane, Lara and Fred stepped out of the aircraft. Climbing down off the wing, they were paraded outside with guns trained on them. Seoras wondered what would happen.

He was pushed down onto his knees, hands tied behind his back. Jane as well. Lara was pushed down onto her face and told to stay there, arms and feet now tied up, along with Fred. Clearly, they had a level of danger above Seoras and Jane.

The sun was warm, and Seoras wanted his fedora, which was back in the aircraft that he'd clambered out of. His hands had been half raised, and he had nothing to hold it with. He'd have to retrieve it after this was all done.

After this is all done, he thought, *will we be done? Will we be going anywhere?*

214

For ten minutes he knelt along the side of the dusty runway, and then a small cavalcade of cars arrived. In the middle was a Rolls Royce, and he watched as it pulled up alongside and the white-suited Wainwright stepped out. He still had a carnation in his suit breast pocket.

'You're quite the adventurers, aren't you?' he said, walking over to Seoras and Jane. 'Quite something, I have to say. I didn't think you would be like this. I didn't think you could keep us running for so long. These two? Well, I don't know how you got involved with them. Or what on earth they're doing, but they clearly can handle themselves.

'We found that out last night. Several of my men are, well, retired. But as for getting out of here—why do you think I have this island? It's difficult to get away from. It's not easy to leave. Unless you have a small army.

'I'm sorry that you saw what you saw,' he said to Jane. 'Quite an enticing woman. And you spent most of your life putting criminals behind bars. Not a good way to go, accidentally seeing something go wrong. Seeing a man being shot at night, paying for it. Must have frustrated you,' said Wainwright. 'Not being able to do what you would have done at home. You could have called several people. In fact, you did send out, didn't you? Otherwise, how would you know about the jewel? You wouldn't have known when you came here. You're not in that line of work. Although you did front up an arts team back in Inverness; is that correct? North of Scotland?'

'And they know we've looked into it,' said Seoras. 'Somebody will come.'

'They won't come. The UK won't be bothered here,' said Wainwright.

'I'm not talking about the government,' said Seoras. 'I have

215

friends. And some of my friends will stop at nothing. If I don't come back from here, they will come for you. They will come to find out, and when they do, well, I will pity you.'

'Don't turn into the big-word bravado man now,' said Wainwright. 'It's gone, it's done. All that's left to do is to finish you. We'll do it quietly, of course; we will not shoot you here. I'll escort you into my car; you'll be taken somewhere. A little accident will happen, so nobody will think any differently.'

'They will,' said Seoras. But he knew the game was up. The likes of Kirsten, even some of the former team, might come to avenge him. Find out what happened to him. But they couldn't stop what was about to happen now. He looked across at Jane. They'd only just got started together. Only just got going on this life after work. Now it was ending. She was smiling at him, but it was a sad smile. There was a tear in her eye. But she was smiling at him. And then Seoras heard something.

It was a whipping sound, like a—yes, blades. Blades in the air. It was a helicopter, wasn't it? But it was a loud helicopter. He looked up, and dots in the distance were suddenly becoming a lot larger. Wainwright turned and looked. Two helicopters arrived but they weren't the sort you got on at the airport. They were heavily armoured, and they looked like they were military.

In the middle of the two of them, however, was a civilian helicopter. It didn't seem to have any weapons and it landed just shy of everyone on the runway. Seoras watched as the door slid back, and Eamon jumped out.

He was wearing trousers and a shirt, had sunglasses on, and had an enormous smile across his face. The two military helicopters, however, remained in the air, but their weapons pointed at the little gathering.

'Wainwright,' said Eamon. 'I think my friends will leave now.'

'Oh, I can't let them leave,' said Wainwright.

'I think you can,' said Eamon. 'These two helicopters behind me belong to Prince Assam of Saudi Arabia. He's not happy that you stole from him. Actually you didn't, but you have what is his. You've killed the man who stole it, but it was always coming to you. You will let these people and our two young friends on the ground get up and walk into this helicopter. The helicopter will then leave. You will then give back the jewel that you stole.'

'I don't have it, do I?'

'You haven't taken it off them yet,' said Eamon. He looked over at Jane. She was smiling. Seoras wasn't smiling because he wasn't sure where this was going. Were they just about to jump out of the frying pan into the fire? Well, the frying pan was certain doom. He'd have to see what the fire was like.

Eamon walked over and untied Jane's hands. The sound of the military helicopters still loud. Dust blew, and Eamon then walked over to Seoras to undo his hands. He motioned at some guards to remove the bonds on the young couple lying on the ground, and Wainwright nodded.

'We will leave,' said Eamon. 'You will not come near Prince Assam's belongings again. You will not set foot anywhere near his companies, his lands, or anything to do with him. If you do, these helicopters will come back and lay waste to this place.'

He turned, walked to Jane and took her hand. 'Come,' he said, 'into the helicopter.'

But she pulled away and walked over to Seoras, taking his hand and kissing him. He broke off after a moment and told her to wait, disappearing inside the hangar and retrieving his hat. Jane shook her head, and then laughed, before walking to the helicopter. Inside the helicopter, they strapped in, the young couple sitting opposite them. Eamon got in last, still smiling, though sporting a large bruise at the top of his head. The helicopter lifted, and they left the island, disappearing into the early morning around them.

Chapter 25

J ane lay back, soaking up the blistering sun. In the distance, she could see the gigantic building. It was incredible, maybe eighty-five stories. She'd seen it on the TV but now, even at this distance, it was impressive.

Her hand reached around the cold tumbler, and she drank the cocktail prepared for her by the personal barman in the corner. He was quite good-looking, in fact, but the man she wanted, the man she had her eyes on, sat in a pair of swimming trunks, looking rather nervous.

He had the fedora hat on his head, the one that had been bought for him by his colleagues when he left the police force. And it seemed now to be something that he was deeply attached to. He didn't like the hot sun. He didn't enjoy lying in it. But he seemed happy. They had spent a couple of days now recuperating and recovering none the wiser about what had happened.

No one had told them anything. But Eamon had disappeared, as had the young couple. Jane wondered what would happen? They couldn't do anything, of course. They were in Dubai, which Seoras had said was a good thing. After all, they hadn't gone back to Saudi Arabia.

So, the prince, who'd owned the jewel, hadn't wanted to see them. Or would he be appearing now, in this hotel complex? Jane had never seen such elegance. And she could get used to it, except for this nervousness, this wonder about what was in the future. She glanced over at Seoras every now and again.

But he still had a worried look on his face. And she could see the mind rolling, thinking. And then there was a familiar cry.

'Oh, top of the morning to you both. How are we today? Feeling better?'

'I wondered when you'd show up,' said Seoras.

'Manners,' said Jane.

'I'll mind my manners when I have the truth.'

'And I'll have a beer,' said Eamon, waving his hand over at the barman in the corner. He pulled up a chair at a table close by and then pointed to the two seats beside it. 'Please, come. I think it's time I had a word with you. Tell you what's going on.'

Seoras stood up, put on a shirt, and then took Jane's hand and led her over, pulling a chair out for her before sitting down. The beer arrived, and Eamon took a deep drink of it, and then pointed to Seoras.

'You're not drinking. I see Jane's got something to keep her going.'

'What's the deal?' asked Seoras.

'The deal?' said Eamon. 'What do you mean, the deal?'

'What are you going to do with us? We know quite a bit. We know a lot. What's going to happen to us?'

'Well,' said Eamon, 'you'll be here for another week, maybe two.'

'And then what?'

'Well, I assume you've got a home to go to,' said Eamon. 'I mean, you could stay for a month, if you want. I'm sure we could foot the bill for that. But you can head home.'

Seoras looked at him. 'What do you mean?'

'Well, I apologise for leaving you here for a couple of days, but I had to see my boss. Prince Assam is my boss. He's quite delighted with the two of you. Astounded, in fact. I'd been there for nearly three years, watching Wainwright. I'm Assam's man. And we knew Wainwright was building something. And we knew he was stashing away treasures. He's taken from many people who live here in the Middle East. Well, we don't take too kindly to that. So, I was asked to investigate, and when I started realising that things were going on there, I got some helpers in. Lara and Fred, I think they called themselves.'

'So you were working with them,' said Seoras.

'I knew something was up when they started coming after you. Wainwright's people. That woman. She'd been used before to dispose of people who'd found things out. I played a long game with that. They didn't suspect me. But I needed somebody to come in and operate. Who, if they got caught, could get out quick leaving me in. Which is why my young friends were there. You, however, caused him a problem. Jane saw our friend get shot. You played the game very well,' said Eamon. 'Not sure what she saw. I take it, Jane, you told him straight away.'

'I didn't know at first,' she said, 'but yes, as soon as I did, I told Seoras.'

'And Detective Chief Inspector Macleod is too clever to just run and tell people. He's in a country where he doesn't have any jurisdiction and he doesn't have any friends.'

'So, you watched us. You watched us. That's how you knew

221

I'd been crabbing. That's how you knew where to be. And then you got your young friends to stay close to us.'

'Yes, I did. Good job too. Hole in the boat. Pulled you out of that one. Nearly got yourselves caught trying to break into a compound. Got you out of that one. What is it? Retirement is just not what it should be? Missing the excitement?'

'I'm missing nothing,' said Seoras. 'I got dragged into this.'

'You did somewhat, didn't you? And then you couldn't get yourself out of it. I'm sorry I had to put the gun on you, but I didn't know how you'd react. Prince Assam wanted that jewel back. Family heirloom, if you wish. It means a lot to him. If you'd have given me the jewel, I would have turned round with the boat, sailed away, dropped you off.'

'Told you,' said Jane. Seoras shook his head.

'In fact, we probably would have paid for plane tickets to take you back to Scotland. You might even have got a thank you from him. As it was, you two gave me a rather severe bump on the head.'

'Well, I'm sorry,' said Seoras, 'but put a gun in my face, and it's what I do. Maybe you should try the truth next time.'

'And you would have believed that?' asked Eamon.

'No,' said Seoras. 'I never know how to play these games. It's why I never joined our secret service. Why I never joined those who did the undercover work, who do the masterly manipulation between states.'

'No, you didn't. I think that's a mistake,' said Eamonn.

'No, it's not. He's alive, and he's here,' said Jane. 'He's too decent a man to do that stuff.'

'Fair enough,' said Eamon.

'One thing I don't understand, though,' said Seoras. 'How did you know? How did you know where we were when we went on the run? You kept appearing. You kept turning up. I took the photograph. You were there when I ran away from the grave. How did you know where we were?'

'If Jane gives me her phone, I'll have that removed. I was tracking you. Jane left the phone on the boat, which was a bit of a mistake.'

'No, it wasn't,' said Jane. 'That's how I got your satellite messages, and we got communication back. It's how we found out about the jewel. It's how we found out about Prince Assam.'

'Ah, I wondered how you knew. It seemed a bit much, just to stumble upon it. Should have known. A bit of detective work, then.'

'Not just me,' said Seoras.

'Well, Prince Assam is delighted with you. He's asked me to convey his thanks. And as such, you're welcome to stay here for the next week, two weeks. If you want to make it a month or two, you can stay. There are many clothing shops. He has left a large tab. You are to furnish your collection and dress yourselves however you want. Your flight back, first class to the UK, will be paid for, and if you ever have need of him again, he has asked me to say that you are more than welcome to place a call to him.'

'Really?' said Seoras.

'Really,' confirmed Eamon. 'That jewel had been missing for the best part of two and a half years. We didn't even know who had taken it. We knew it would come. And then, the man who brought it was killed. We didn't know who he truly was, not until you took the photo, of course. They guessed he was involved, but I hadn't seen him.'

'Well, we heard him on the island. You weren't that good.'

'No, he was good. He kept out of the way,' said Eamon.

223

'Chances are you probably overheard him by luck. But I'll be off now. There's a credit card waiting inside your bedroom. Use it for everything. There's no limit.'

'No limit?' said Seoras.

'No limit. I told you who I work for,' said Eamon. 'The value of the jewel you recovered for him is beyond priceless. Not in a monetary sense; it's part of the family; it's part of their heritage. I'm sure you have somebody back there who could tell you about that. Considering you ran an arts department, you don't seem to know much about the arts.'

'I didn't run it, I oversaw it,' said Seoras. 'And no, I know little about it, if I'm honest. Just a piece of rock.'

'If you ever meet him,' said Eamon, 'don't tell him that, okay? It's a piece of rock that pays my wages, though.' He stood up, came over to Jane, took her hand to shake it and then bent down and kissed her on the cheek. 'One of the nicest women I've ever met,' he said. 'If you ever bore of him, look me up.'

'You're outrageous,' said Jane. 'What makes you think he could ever bore me?'

'Well, let's see how much he lets you put on that credit card,' said Eamon. He turned and shook Seoras's hand. 'No hard feelings over our little skirmish.'

'Well, thank you for looking after us, saving our lives. Several times, I guess.'

'It benefited us both. Please spend on that card. He won't even notice it.'

Seoras stood watching Eamon disappear and then felt Jane stand up beside him. She slipped her arms around him.

'An entire week, two, maybe, a month.'

'I am not staying here for a month. It's too bloomin' hot.'

'Take you shopping, though. I can buy you new stuff. Yes?

We can get you a whole new wardrobe. You can be fashionable.'

'I am fashionable,' said Seoras. He put the fedora on his head again and walked over to stand at the railings at the balcony that looked out over Dubai.

'Where do you want to go?' asked Jane.

'Where do we want to go? I thought we were going back to Inverness.'

'He's given us that card to spend whatever we want on it; we could book our next holiday. They've got travel agents here, haven't they?'

'I can't do that. That's just abusing the man. That's just—'

'No, it's not,' said Jane. 'We nearly paid with our lives for looking after this jewel. Once, twice, three times maybe. We were almost killed. He owes us a couple of holidays. In fact, let's book a few. You don't want clothes. I don't want diamonds and necklaces and all that. But we said we were going to enjoy our retirement. Go places. Well then, let him pay for it. If he's that thankful for what we've done for him, and he's got the money, let him pay for it.'

'Okay,' said Seoras, 'but we go somewhere cooler, somewhere in the mountains.'

'Okay, you choose the first one, I'll choose the second one, you can choose the third, and I choose the fourth.'

'How many holidays are you going to book on the man?'

'As many as it takes. Eamon said he wouldn't even notice the expense; these guys are worth millions. You've worked your whole life, Seoras, you have put yourself in dangerous situations, and we deserve it. Do you not think? Do you not think I deserve it? Leave him behind. Leave the detective behind and let's go on adventures.'

'When I say I want adventure, I don't want to be hunted

down. I don't want to be chasing around the globe and have people with guns pointing at me. I want the adventure to be you,' said Seoras. 'You're the adventure. You're everything.'

'You're really corny when you're serious; do you know that?'

'Well, I don't have the charm.'

'That's where you're wrong,' said Jane. 'When you're straight-forward and you're honest, that's when you have charm. I know I'm the adventure you want. That's why I'm here. Let's have some. You and me. Seoras and Jane. Let's go explore this world.'

She pulled close to him, wrapped her arms around him, and then found he had slipped behind her. His arms were around her waist, and she felt him nuzzling into her neck.

'Okay,' he said. 'But don't lose that card.'

'Do you think he'll want it back? Do you think we can keep it when we leave here?'

'I think you're going to try.'

She looked up at him, smiled, and then she grimaced suddenly.

'You're seeing him, aren't you?' said Seoras, pulling her tight. 'You'll learn to live with it. He may never leave your thoughts, but we can pay for people now to help you. You'll learn to live with it.'

She kissed him. 'Help me.'

About the Author

GR Jordan is a self-published author who finally decided at forty that in order to have an enjoyable lifestyle, his creative beast within would have to be unleashed. His books mirror that conflict in life where acts of decency contend with self-promotion, goodness stares in horror at evil, and kindness blindsides us when we at our worst. Corrupting our world with his parade of wondrous and horrific characters, he highlights everyday tensions with fresh eyes whilst taking his methodical, intelligent mainstays on a roller-coaster ride of dilemmas, all the while suffering the banter of their provocative sidekicks.

A graduate of Loughborough University where he masqueraded as a chemical engineer but ultimately played American football, Gary had worked at changing the shape of cereal flakes and pulled a pallet truck for a living. Watching vegetables freeze at -40'C was another career highlight and he was also one of the Scottish Highlands "blind" air traffic controllers.

These days he has graduated to answering a telephone to people in trouble before telephoning other people to sort it out.

Having flirted with most places in the UK, he is now based in the Isle of Lewis in Scotland where his free time is spent between raising a young family with his wife, writing, figuring out how to work a loom and caring for a small flock of chickens. Luckily, his writing is influenced by his varied work and life experience as the chickens have not been the poetical inspiration he had hoped for!

You can connect with me on:

🌐 https://www.grjordan.com

📘 https://facebook.com/carpetlessleprechaun

Also by G R Jordan

G R Jordan writes across multiple genres including crime, dark and action adventure fantasy, feel good fantasy, mystery thriller and horror fantasy. Below is a selection of his work. Whilst all books are available across online stores, signed copies are available at his personal shop.

Seoras, Save The Kid! (Seoras Macleod Mysteries #2)
https://grjordan.com/product/seroas-2
On top of the world — with a child to call your own!

Former DCI Seoras Macleod and his partner Jane are chasing nostalgia aboard a historic steam train cutting through the majestic Alps. But their peaceful journey is shattered when a daring kidnap attempt unfolds before their eyes. Seoras steps in — and instantly becomes the kidnappers' new target.

Steam, steel, and secrets collide in a high-altitude race across Europe. All aboard — before the boiler blows!

Lonely at the Top (Highlands & Islands Detective Thrillers #51)
https://grjordan.com/product/lonely-at-the-top

An elite businessman is found dead at the top of the Cairngorms. A solitary life leads to no clues about a motive. In her first case after Macleod's retirement can Hope deliver as her new DCI questions if she really can cut the mustard?

In the wake of DCI Macleod's retirement, DI Hope McGrath inherits a new DCI, one who doesn't hold with the glamourous image Hope has within the force. When a man without enemies is brutally killed atop the Cairngorms, Hope feels the pressure as she is harangued over every move she makes by her new boss. With her young boy pining for Mum, and her partner struggling at home, can Hope rise above the distractions and pressure to understand who wants the perfect hermit dead?

The quiet life is merely turbulence in the shadows!

Kirsten Stewart Thrillers
https://grjordan.com/product/a-shot-at-democracy
Join Kirsten Stewart on a shadowy ride through the underbelly of the Highlands of Scotland where among the beauty and splendour of the majestic landscape lies corruption and intrigue to match any city. From murders to extortion, missing children to criminals operating above the law, the Highland former detective must learn a tougher edge to her work as she puts her own life on the line to protect those who cannot defend themselves.

Having left her beloved murder investigation team far behind, Kirsten has to battle personal tragedy and loss while adapting to a whole new way of executing her duties where your mistakes are your own. As Kirsten comes to terms with working with the new team, she often operates as the groups solo field agent, placing herself in danger and trouble to rescue those caught on the dark side of life. With action packed scenes and tense scenarios of murder and greed, the Kirsten Stewart thrillers will have you turning page after page to see your favourite Scottish lass home!

There's life after Macleod, but a whole new world of death!

Jac's Revenge (A Jac Moonshine Thriller #1)

https://grjordan.com/product/jacs-revenge

An unexpected hit makes Debbie a widow. The attention of her man's killer spawns a brutal yet classy alter ego. But how far can you play the game before it takes over your life?

All her life, Debbie Parlor lived in her man's shadow, knowing his work was never truly honest. She turned her head from news stories and rumours. But when he was disposed of for his smile to placate a rival crime lord, Jac Moonshine was born. And when Debbie is paid compensation for her loss like her car was written off, Jac decides that enough is enough.

Get on board with this tongue-in-cheek revenge thriller that will make you question how far you would go to avenge a loved one, and how much you would enjoy it!

 **A Giant Killing (Siobhan Duffy Mysteries #1)**
https://grjordan.com/product/a-giant-killing
A body lies on the Giant's boot. Discord, as the master of secrets has been found. Can former spy Siobhan Duffy find the killer before they execute her former colleagues?

When retired operative Siobhan Duffy sees the killing of her former master in the paper, her unease sends her down a path of discovery and fear. Aided by her young housekeeper and scruff of a gardener, Siobhan begins a quest to discover the reason for her spy boss' death and unravels a can of worms today's masters would rather keep closed. But in a world of secrets, the difference between revenge and simple, if brutal, housekeeping becomes the hardest truth to know.

The past is a child who never leaves home!